Wanting
Eyes

ISBN   978-0-578-00837-0

Printed in the United States of America.

Preface

Everyone wants to be loved. Trusting, monogamous, nurturing love that inspires us to different heights, and encompasses our soul. Through my experiences and experiences of others, males and females alike, WANTING EYES was created. It was created to let men and women know that we both share the same wants, but past experiences haunt us that we have to overcome to find that true love or that soul mate.

WANTING EYES was also created to inform women that there are still good men out there, hardworking and faithful with lots of love to give. Don't let bad experiences spoil your search for true love. Don't give up searching.

"Love starts from the love you have for yourself. That love is reflected in how you act, carry yourself, and through your interactions with people you meet. The attraction is what you reflect, the choices is from what you believe."

Ron Broussard

Acknowledgements

Acknowledgements are given to my Supreme Being for giving me the gift to write and show sensitivity. Further acknowledgments are given to my mother who was my first teacher on love and gave invaluable advice on finding true love. To all the women I have loved before, a part of you lives inside of me today. To my sisters, who through their experiences gave me the inspiration to write.

I dedicate this novel to my soul mate Michiyo, that through her, I was taught a new meaning of true love, that I had given up on years ago.

"There is a destiny that makes us brothers: No one goes his way alone. All that we send into the lives of others comes back into our own"

Psalms 1 "Blessed is the man and the woman who have grown beyond themselves and have seen through their separations."
"They delight in the way things are and keep their hearts open, day and night."
"They are like trees planted near flowing rivers, which bear fruit when they are ready their leaves will not fall or wither."
 -The book of Psalms
Adapted by Stephen Michell

1

PIERRE

He was going to pick them up Saturday evening. It had been difficult without her. He stood in the living room and surveyed the apartment. In baggy jeans and a tank top T-shirt, he looked surprisingly boyish and rugged. He was a handsome man; smooth coffee cream colored skin, long lean runners legs; flat taut abdomen, defined back and biceps; strong hands. Pierre was perfectly made and as male as they came. His bald head, nicely shaved, accented his broad shoulders and chest that bulged from his T-shirt. His brown eyes blazed with excitement because he was picking his babies up from his in-laws across town, but cleaning was inevitable. The apartment was strewn with clothes from morning to evening. The dishes, so many dirty, made it hard to spot the clean ones. Were they gone just a week? He busied himself around the apartment, washing and cleaning. By the time he finished, his body was tired and weak.

Pierre walked over to the window, picked up his glass of water on the way, and took long, deep gulps while he stared out at the city of Atlanta. The lights of the skyscrapers sparkled through the fingers of fog that was slowly creeping across the city. He loved this town, the crowded streets, the bicycle messengers dodging between cars, the honking horns, the delicious smells coming from every restaurant; from the Italian restaurants to the mysterious Far East scents emanating from the Chinese and Thai restaurants in Buckhead.

Pierre drew in a long, tired sigh and sat down slowly. He really does procrastinate. Kim had been on his case ever since they were married. Maybe she was right. Maybe it was time to stop putting things off till the last minute. Still, it is hard to break habits. He glanced at the clock, six-thirty. She would complain all the way to the east side if he wasn't prompt, if not earlier.

The apartment was spotless; He knew she would be proud of that as he locked the door, then hurried himself down the hall to the elevator. He wondered why everything goes so slow when you're in a rush?. The elevator came to a halt with a ring and the doors opened. He hurried to his car and got in. The engine purred to life as he turned the key. Right now, on a stormy evening in mid April, Pierre wanted to be anywhere but on the road, headed to his in-laws. He tried to make his wife stay till the weather cleared up, but she made him promise to pick her up regardless. He was missing them though. He couldn't go another day without having his wife near, his three year old son Jeremy wanting to play, asking him endless question after question like a learning sponge, soaking knowledge.

He turned up in his in-laws driveway, ten minutes early and happy. This will only take a couple of minutes, he thought as he saw Jeremy banging on the window, waving happily as he strode up the sidewalk to embrace his wife.

"How'd the week go?" Pierre asked.

Terrible Kim had been tempted to answer, but instead mumbled something about it was okay, that is, if you call being told how to care for your own son great.

PIERRE

"Baby, you wanted to stay for a week." Pierre said with a grin as they started arm in arm up the sidewalk.

"Daddy!" exclaimed Jeremy as he pushed the screen door to let them in, then hugged his father's leg.

"Did you miss me?" Asked Pierre.

"Nope," Jeremy said as Pierre picked him up and set him on his shoulders.

"Grandpa took me to the toy store and the zoo and he-

"And he spoiled you rotten that's what he did," Pierre said as he kissed grandma on the cheek. "Where's grandpa?"

"Out getting somethin sweet," she sighed sadly. "I told him bout goin out in this kinda weather. You sure your not gonna stay at least till it calms down?"

"Well, they've worn out their welcome," Pierre said as Kim nudged him in the back.

"Besides, Kim interrupted, you have to come to the East side once in a while to visit, get away from the suburbs for a spell."

"Well, I do need a change of scenery," Grandma said as she fixed her apron. "You think grandpa will let me?"

"Yeah Ma, he'll let you," Kim said, as she gave her a hug. "Tell grandma bye Jeremy."

"Bye grandma," Jeremy said as Pierre lifted him off his shoulders to her outstretched arms.

"Bye, bye baby. You be good to mommy and daddy and grandma will have something special when I come," she promised as she kissed and hugged him, then put him down.

"Okay," Jeremy said as he tried to head for the door.

"Wait!" Kim said sternly, grabbing him by the arm. "Wait till daddy opens the car doors for us, you wanna catch cold?"

"Yeah, let daddy do the dirty work," Pierre said as he embraced grandma, then headed out the door.

"Be careful!" grandma shouted as they hurried to the car when Pierre motioned for them.

5

******

"I'll give your mom a week and she'll be at our door," Pierre said as he watched Kim strap Jeremy in his car seat, then herself, making sure her seat belt was comfortable.

"Grandmas will be grandmas, she said with a sigh. "Did you miss me?"

"Miss you? I couldn't wait till Saturday came," he said as he reached over and kissed her. "When we get home, I'll put Jeremy to sleep, put some soft jazz on the stereo, and pour us a little white wine and we'll have with some chocolate covered strawberries, and I'll go into detail about how much I missed you"

Kim looked up at him with soft eyes for a moment, then back to her moving fingers.

"That sounds nice," she said gently, rubbing his thigh as they eased out of the driveway.

Suddenly a car, speeding recklessly, blurred in their sight as their car rolled backward and, before they could blink their eyes, slammed into their Maxima. And, with the grinding of metal and screeching of brakes, everything went blank.

PIERRE

****

Pierre was never to forget the expression on his wife's face. Happy and content, her eyes full of love. The look on his son's face was what Pierre remembered the most; Happy, bright-eyed with excitement.

He awoke in a hospital room, quiet, except for his parents, in-laws and friends whispering amongst themselves.

"What happened!" He cried as he rose up in bed only to be held by his parents.
"A drunk driver, said his mother. Speeding, wouldn't slow down."
She repeated it over and over, sobbing like a frightened child, tears flowing down her cheeks. Then finally before his father hugged her, she cried out, "He killed them!"

Pierre fell back in bed, shocked, the room spinning, tears came to his eyes as his mother and father hugged him. They knew he wouldn't get over it.

Two weeks later, they buried Kim and Jeremy in the Burrelson Cemetery. Seems like yesterday they were together. When his mother asked to talk and try to get over it; he told her he could never get over it, that he could never love again.

3:30 p.m.; Atlanta, Georgia; 1994

2

PIERRE

Pierre sat down at his computer and got it up and working. His mind was not into working though, his eyes were fixed, as though he was searching.

He worked as a technical illustrator at a very prominent advertising company, Burke and Burke. The Burke and Burke Concord building was located in the sprawling metropolis district of Midtown, Atlanta's business and historic heart of the city. His corner office had a beautiful view of the downtown area as far as the eye could see. He could see traffic winding down Fourteenth Street, and in the distance highway 75/85 winding by downtown in a sprawling snakelike fashion. Head of the technical sales division, he ran it smoothly, making sure all of the projects were completed before the deadline. He enjoyed his work, from the meetings to showing and demonstrating a client's new product, to providing the necessary advisory services to all clientele, including his bosses' weekly updates on the current projects.

WANTING EYES

Raised from a family of six siblings, he worked hard to be the best at everything he wanted to accomplish. And he was, graduating from high school with top honors and was granted a four year scholarship at the University of Georgia. There he met Kim, a short, chocolate brown sista going to college on an athletic scholarship. They hit it off very well and she was his sweetheart through college.

Inspired by her, she pushed him to do things he wouldn't have had the spirit to continue. Now, just as she suddenly came into his life, she was gone, leaving sweet memories embedded in his soul. He gazed out of the window in his office on the twelfth floor and watched people walk gaily, rushing to and fro, from the subterranean marketplaces with its shops, bars, and cafes; to other buildings that matched the Concord building in height and stature, for meetings, briefings and conferences. Midtown was a live, breathing, business beast that held everyone in its clutches from nine to five. The phone rang, interrupting his thoughts.

"Burke and Burke Advertising Company," he said calmly over the phone.
"Yo, nigga what's up? Down for the move or what?" Marcus asked.

Marcus was in his early thirties. He was a short guy, medium build with coffee cream colored skin and thick dark curly hair that he wore in a flattop. His birthmark was a blond patch of hair that was noticeable even when he cuts his hair low. His eyebrows were thick, accented by his light brown eyes.

He was a ladies man- or so he thought. He schemed on most of his women through his freelance photography business. Though his photo gigs came a little less than the women, he always talked about hitting it big with a modeling company or a magazine.

"Yeah, I'm down," Pierre replied, puzzled at the abrupt change of thought.

"Are you okay? You sound distant."

"Yeah, I'm all right, just thinking."

"Yo man, it is too late to start thinking now, you'll like living there. You need to start thinking about all the women living around you."

"Yeah, there are some women there."

"Check it, I'll be over in an hour or so, okay? Peace."

"Peace."

Marcus seemed excited. But Pierre didn't care. He always thought about himself when women were involved. Pierre always wondered why they often hung together. They were two different guys.   Pierre believed in treating women right and Marcus was a player. That is what probably drew them together in high school. They had totally different perspectives towards women. Marcus believes in ratio and proportion, meaning the female-to-male ratio in Atlanta was seven to one. And it was easy to have multiple relationships because the women were so desperate for companionship, and more than a few of them were willing to share a man as long as they had access to occasional sex and someone to go out with. And with the brothers that were more plentiful than any woman could possibly imagine, what most women didn't realize was that the majority of them were either married, bisexual, gay, or just plain playing the field for all they could get out of it, making easy pickings for a single black male that is career oriented with a stable job and no kids, all the more alluring. Marcus would learn, though. You will never find a good women if you are treating them wrong. You will always run into the wrong ones that will use you for what you have until you have no more, then move on.

Pierre got up from his desk and moved to his illustrator table where the latest project was ready for his review. He looked over their final work. Everything must be perfect for the presentation he has to give for the Copeland account. He browsed over it carefully as the phone rang.

"Burke and Burke Advertising Company."
"Hey, need some help? I get off at three." Rob suggested.

Rob was also in his early thirties. He was tall, about 6'2, with a slender build and smooth, mocha dark skin. His hair was black as coal and he wore it with dreadlocks on top and faded on the sides. Thick eyebrows and eyelashes accented his deep brown eyes. His nose was large with flared nostrils that sat on top of a neatly trimmed thick mustache. Big, full lips that most women would just love to let him kiss them all over their body.

He married his college sweetheart Marie, two years after the accident Pierre had. His son Christian was smarter than the average five year old.

Rob was a registered nurse working at the Crawford Long Hospital, located several blocks away from the Concord building. He often talked about the flirtatious nurses at his job trying to give him some play, but Marcus and I knew he wouldn't do anything. I could always count on him to give good sound advice. Marcus had his own ideas about life in general. Marcus, Rob and I bonded closer after the accident, like brothers that none of us had.

"Yeah, I can always use extra hands. Did Marcus call you?"
"Fifteen minutes ago. I'm getting ready to raise up."
"Cool, meet us at Stonehenge townhouses at five-thirty, bet?"

"Bet, see ya there, Peace."
"Peace."

Pierre finished his work at the table, glancing at the clock in the process. This might be more than we can accomplish, he thought. He cleared his desk, turned off the computer, grabbed his wind breaker, and was off.

He walked down the corridor, whistling as he went. He was glad his friends was helping him, they were always there when he needed them, as the elevators doors sprung open invitingly. He walked in and pushed buttons. The elevator groaned slightly as it made its descent. A porter in the parking complex pulled up in his shiny black Lexus coupe. He purchased the car four years after he received his insurance settlement. Rob and Marcus had hammered him day after day about punishing himself like it was his fault, so he purchased it to make them think he was getting over that fateful day. But nothing could replace them, it only reminded him as he and the porter exchanged places.

He drove, straight out of the basement parking complex and headed immediately south down Peachtree Street toward his new home. Only thirty minutes away would be an easy commute, he thought as he was cruising, listening to some soft jazz.

Within minutes he pulled up at his townhouse complex. There on time was Rob and Marcus, arguing as usual. Marcus was always teasing Rob about him not having a life cause he was married and Rob was countering by stating Marcus wasn't the "player" that he thought he was. Pierre was always the mediator, but today he didn't feel the need for it.

"Have the movers came yet?" Pierre inquired, stepping out of the car.

"No, you know it will be a while, they're on CP time (colored peoples time), and they get paid by the hour," Rob replied, without even glancing at him, still upset with Marcus's comment.

"Cool, you can come check it," Pierre continued as he started up the stairs.

"The new crib."

They followed him up the stairs to his apartment, joking as they went. As they opened the door, their heads nodded approvingly. The apartment was beautiful.

The floors were pure oak with matching panel midway on the walls. The entrance vestibule was marble floor lowered, with sliding doors leading to the patio. It had three steps that lead to the raised living room. The living room was endless, sprawling expanse of deep rich hardwood floors, complete with a fireplace on the center wall. To the right of the fireplace was three steps leading to the raised bedroom and a small hallway leading to the kitchen, which also had sliding doors to the patio. The patio had a wood fence surrounding the small backyard that offered a great view of Atlanta's skyline.

"I need this crib," observed Marcus as he walked in the living room. "You know how many females will be turned on by just seeing this. They'll come in, see this place, get dizzy, and end up in bed, your bed and that's it, you're bonin." Marcus stated gesturing with his hand was clenched fist, motioning back and forth.

"Yeah, you can pull a nice female with this place," Rob added, agreeing with Marcus.

"And that's what you need."

"What I need is a woman to accept me for me," Pierre explained, peering out the window watching the movers pull up.

"If it is meant for me to find someone special, it will happen, and I wouldn't have to be hooked up with blind dates. We'll both know we're meant to be."

"I hope you find her before you bust," teased Marcus, grabbing his crotch. "How long has it been anyway?"

"Long enough," Pierre stated calmly. "I just hope I'm ready when this miraculous event occurs."

"Yo, your ready for Rob, me, you, and a couple mo' niggas with that buildup," added Marcus jokingly, grabbing himself. "Let's hope she's ready."

"Let's hope your ready to tote these boxes," Pierre countered, glancing out the window as he headed for the door. "The movers just pulled up. Let's go."

3

SANDRA

Sandra Bell was quiet this Thursday afternoon. Instead of the usual frenzied men and women and children coming in and out of the office, the patrons today were more relaxed, less stressed, and content to perusing the magazines in the waiting room. While sometimes Sandra needed the hectic pace of the work week to meet her bills, she couldn't help enjoying the leisurely pace of Thursdays.

The only drawback of today's slow influx of customers was that she had too much time to think - about all the past men in her life. Thankfully she had some work to do or she would daydream and ponder the ongoing thought she has had for years; *where can a sista find a decent man?*

The doctor's office was nice and clean, with the exception of a few patients' records and appointment slips strewn about on Sandra's desk. After I finish doing his appointment book and filing these records, I'm gone thought Sandra as she penciled in entry after entry. She glanced out the window briefly, the continued her work. I should be able to catch a few rays before sunset, she thought. Sandra loved sunning, especially when she didn't have to work the next day. Dr. Silberman always gave her Fridays off.

Sandra was a beautiful, petite woman in her late twenties

with caramel brown skin, light brown eyes, and natural sandy red curly hair that she wore in a chin length bob with shorter earlobe-length layers curly on her crown. She has a sexy, raspy voice. When she smiled, she looked like she just did something mischievous. Very athletic, she played softball and worked out occasionally. Her body was very tone and taut to perfection, also silky smooth from her taking lots of bubble baths. She could make men stop and stare while they were WITH their wives.

Very independent, she is a person that wanted to be in control all the time; in her work, social and personal relationships. But she would succumb if she found a good man that could control her.

She finished her appointment book then got up to start filing patients' records when the phone rang. Damn! She thought, almost finished and somebody always calls when you're about to leave.

"Dr. Silberman's office may I help you?" She said flatly on the phone, trying to maintain her cool.

"Hey girlfriend, caught you when your trying to leave, didn't I?" said Monique, laughing on the phone.

Monique was a pretty, mocha complexion woman that wore her long curly black hair one-length; a shoulder-skimming bob with shorter earlobe to chin layers razzored around her face. She thought it made her look intelligent. She has a slender face with deep, dark black eyes and high cheek bones. A little voluptuous than Sandra, she always teased her about gaining weight. Monique and Sandra were good friends despite the constant gossip and advice that she so willingly tries to give. She dated many men, and loved at least one thing about them all. It was just difficult for her to decide which one was better for her. Sandra always told her that if they ever found out about each other, she'd be in a world of trouble.

"Girl, I thought you were another patient with an appointment," said Sandra.

"Yeah, I have an appointment for you to meet a tall, light skinned Zulu with brown eyes, a nice ass, and a fine body."

"Okay, what's wrong with him?"

"What do you mean what's wrong with him?"

"If he's all that, how come you don't want him?"

"He is not my type, besides, I'm already juggling too many. Threes a crowd, you know. I can't handle them as it is now."

"Your last man I met was married, crazy, and broke, how is he?"

"I don't know. I just know he moved into your townhouse complex TODAY."

"Is that so? So I can assume I'll be seeing you after work today, huh?"

"I'll beat you there."

****

Thirty minutes later Sandra pulled up in the townhouse basement parking, secured her car, and headed upstairs. *I wonder what he looks like;* she thought only to run into him, knocking empty boxes and newspapers everywhere.

"I'm terribly sorry," she said, as she started helping him pick up everything.

"It's just trash," Pierre said. "In a rush?"

"No, I was actually thinking about something, not really paying attention." She said shyly.

He is fine, she thought to herself, all that and a bowl of grits*! Tall, muscular, with a bald head and light brown eyes that I can gaze into hours.*

"My name is Pierre Mason. I moved into the empty condo upstairs. And your name is?" he inquired politely, shaking her hand.

"Sandra," she said, remembering her name. "Sandra Belle."

"Pleased to meet you Sandra. I wish we could have got together under better circumstances," he added laughing.

"I agree," she replied, not thinking about what he said.

She was weak-kneed, gazing, but not enough to stare at this black beau. He finished picking up the scattered newspapers and started for the trash bin. She broke out of her trance and followed.

"Once you're settled, would you care to come over for a glass of wine?" She asked question. "Kind of a welcome to the neighborhood drink?"

"Don't mind if I do," Pierre replied as he threw the trash away. "Where do you stay?"

"I live in 307," she explained, gazing into his eyes. "Look forward to seeing you."

He watched her as she walked. *Me too*, he thought. *She's a beautiful woman, but she probably has a man.* He thought nothing of it as he threw the rest of the trash away and went upstairs.

Her body leaned heavily against the door as she let out a big sigh. *He is fine!* She thought. *God must have brought him to me. Boy! I sure hope there aren't any attachments that go with him like ex-wives, excess kids everywhere, or girlfriends.* She walked down the hall to her bedroom, changed into her shorts and a halter top and went out on the patio to sun. It is gonna be a long summer, she thought to herself as the doorbell rang.

"Come in Monique, I'm back here!" Sandra shouted. "Make yourself useful and bring me a drink, I need it."

"You must have seen him," observed Monique as she walked out on the patio and handed her a drink. "Tell me how he looks."

"Like you don't know!" Sandra explained with delight. "He is fine girl, I can get with him. His name is Pierre and I gave him an invitation to come over and have a drink when he is ready."

"So that must be his Lexus," Monique interrupted. "Cause it's personalized with PIERRE on the plates."

"Jackpot!" They exclaimed as they slapped a hi-five in the air.

"I need a man to take care of me," Sandra stated, taking a sip of her drink. "A man and his money."

"Take your time with him girl," Monique suggested. "See where he is going and what he is doing with his life."

"He must be doing a lot, seeing that he has a Lexus," Sandra said flatly.

"You know what I mean. You don't want to hook up with a player, especially when AIDS is large and trying to be in charge. Use protection before giving him anything."

"Yes mother dear," Sandra replied sarcastically. "Anyway, I have to know him before I do anything, and that is exactly what

I'm going to do."

"Whatever," replied Monique, ignoring her. "Just do what I said and stop jumping into relationships legs up and you will be happy, okay? Well, I gotta go. Dexter taking me to the Prime for dinner tonight. Talk to you tomorrow."

But Sandra paid no attention to Monique. She tried to concentrate on what to anticipate from Pierre and came up blank. She would only allow herself to feel lust. Sandra got up from sunning, took a nice, hot bath, then sat down in her favorite chair and listened to some Miles softly. She spent the rest of the evening thinking about making love to him. It made her fall asleep that night having her mind wander, thinking about her last tragic relationship. The idea of loving was not the equation. She didn't want to love anybody, not yet. Right now she couldn't. She was hurt bad from her last relationship and needed someone to help her recover. Love would come later. So she focused on his body. It kept her occupied as she drifted off to sleep, visions of Pierre Mason's muscular body dancing in her head.

The doorbell woke her up Friday morning. She thought she was dreaming at first until it became so persistent she opened one eye and peered at the clock. It was after eleven. When it kept ringing she got up and went to see who it was.

"It's me," said a feminine voice softly. "You know we're doing hair today, get up girl."

Monique.

"I'll be right down," she said.

PIERRE

Pierre walked lazily into the kitchen and made some coffee. The sun shone brightly through the patio doors, warming the kitchen floor. He stood at the patio doors, looking down into his little yard. The apartment was quiet, except for faint ticking of his antique grandfather clock in the corner. He turned away from the patio door and went slowly into the living room. As it always did, being alone and missing them made him feel empty.

The living room was completely furnished and finished. It was done with a series of deep, rich reds and black. The floor was endless, sprawling expanse of deep rich hardwood with the exception of a few Oriental rugs tastefully placed where the least traffic would occur . Beautiful, with a dauntingly, complex, labyrinthine Oriental bazaar of rust, gold, beige and bronze colors, hand woven, laid on the floor, giving the room just a touch of class.

There was no better way for Pierre to spend an afternoon, drinking some wine as he lay on the floor, casually reading a favorite novel. Black art covered every possible square inch of wall space. His place was like a gallery in there with beautiful Asian art dominating the east, and African art dominating the west. The works of the Nsukka group; Beautiful, colorful, engaging pieces of patterns combined prints of long limbed people populated the foyer. The small hall leading to the bedroom was a collage of Songhai and Ghana African masks that were worn by men who portrayed in their time, the mythological role of females. There was a wide screen TV on the right wall facing the window, with a custom made entertainment shelf with his Nakamichi stereo on it. A thick, large, black Persian rug with a mahogany coffee table was in front of the sofa. On it sat many African figurines of idealized African women with their large breasts and wide hips that were displayed, not only for their beauty and ornamental quality, but also for their potent symbolism of the essential strength, vitality, and fertility of African women. The black leather sofa was under the large window that looked out over the neighborhood and the matching love seat was on the far wall facing the fireplace. His Yamaha speakers were on each side of the sofa. His cylinder shaped aquarium, that he prided so much, stood next to the fireplace on an Benin African stool that look like an African woman carrying a large pan on her head, with overhanging lamp above it. The sun shone, trying to creep in through the blinders, making yellow lines on the floor, and the wood felt warm under his bare feet. He picked up a newspaper and sat on the sofa in the silk boxers' shorts he slept in instead of his Charmeause lounge pants, reading. He looked up when the doorbell rang.

"I know he is not still sleep," mumbled a husky voice through the door.

Marcus.

He's up early, thought Pierre as he shuffled to the door.

"Yo man, you're not ready?" said Marcus as he came through the door. "I know you knew we were going to shoot some hoops. We're on the clock, Rob is with us."

"Oh, I forgot," Pierre replied smiling. "I'll be ready in a moment."

Rob's wife always argued about Rob shooting ball with them because he always came home later than the time he tells her. Pierre dashed upstairs to change his clothes as Marcus walked around the apartment.

"You did nice," Marcus nodded approvingly, glancing around the room. "You're only missing one thing."
"What?" Pierre shouted from the bedroom.
"A woman's touch. You can tell a brother is living here, alone. When are you going to stop punishing yourself and start dating?"
"I met someone yesterday," Pierre added, smiling as he walked into the living room half dressed, holding his shoes. "She lives upstairs. Her name is Sandra Bell and she invited me over for a drink."
"And you turned her down I bet," interrupted Marcus, tossing the basketball in the air.
"No," Pierre stated, turning serious. "Actually I took her up on the offer, and as soon I'm comfortable, I'll consider."
"What are you waiting for?" asked Marcus. "How are you going to find someone if you don't give anyone a chance?"
Marcus shook his head, turned, and slowly walked to the door and opened it.
"You need to take a chance, just once," he insisted, standing in the door. "I'll be downstairs."

He turned and closed the door behind him.

What am I waiting on? His thoughts raced through his mind as he put on his sweatshirt. I'll chance it just once , he thought as he left his place, locked the door, then went upstairs. He found himself knocking on Sandra's door.

A beautiful, tall dark skinned woman answered the door.

"Yes, may I help you?" Monique inquired politely, looking surprised.

"Yes, I'm Pierre Mason. I moved into the apartment downstairs two days ago. Is Sandra here?" He asked.

"Yes, she's here. I'm her friend, Monique Grae. Pleased to meet you," she replied, shaking his hand. "She's doing her hair. Come in, I'll get her for you."

She led him into the living room, then went to Sandra's bedroom.

"He's here," Monique whispered excitedly, closing the door quietly. "He's here, in your living room."

"I can't go out there like this girl," explained Sandra, trying to put her hair together with no success.

"Ask him what does he want," Sandra stated, opening the door and pushing her.

"Hi Pierre. I'm between hairstyles," she asked shyly. "What's up?"

"Nothin," he replied, smiling at the sight. "Just stopped by to tell you I'll take you up on that offer that offer that is if you're not too busy? See you at seven?"

"Seven sounds fine," Sandra nodded calmly, trying to keep her cool.

"I'll see you later then," he said, heading for the door. "I have to catch my friends."

"Bye," Sandra replied as she watched him leave.

"Girl, he looks better than my gossip source described him," Monique continued, fanning herself. "She must have seen him from a distance. Are you ready for him, girlfriend?"
"Ready as I'll ever be," Sandra replied, shaking her hips. "I just hope he's ready for me."

Together they laughed as they went back in the bedroom.

With Monique there, Sandra didn't pay much attention to the clock till after she left at two-thirty. Well I guess I'll take a quick nap, she thought as she set her clock for five. Everything has to be perfect when he comes over this evening. First impressions makes lasting ones, she thought as drifted off to sleep.

WANTING EYES

Her alarm clock blared loudly with an annoying ring. Five
o'clock. She woke groggily, glanced at the clock, then jumped
up with start.   *Got to get ready* she thought to herself. She took
a shower, careful not to wet her hair, then thumbed through her
wardrobe looking for just the right thing to wear. She usually
didn't pay much attention about what she wore, but this evening
she wanted to look good. She picked out a beige short set,
springy, but warm enough for chilly April weather. As she put
on her makeup, she realized she was dressing for Pierre. That
embarrassed her. She didn't want him to think she was coming
on strong. At least not yet. She busied herself around the
apartment, setting the mood. A little dim light, here and there,
programs her stereo with jazz, putting the wine on ice. Everything was perfect, she thought as she sat down, listening to the
music to put her in a relaxed mood.

****

When Pierre arrived that evening and rang her doorbell, Sandra was standing outside, gazing at the skyline as the sun hid behind the buildings. Beautiful, she thought as she hurried to the door and peered through the peephole, seeing him, then quickly straightening her clothes and hair. She took a deep breath, then opened the door with a smile.

"Hello, she said with a smile. "You're early."
 He spoke quietly in a soft hypnotic voice. "I'm always on time for everything."
"I see. Come in and make yourself comfortable," she suggested as she led him to the living room.
"I'll be back in a minute with the wine. This is going to be a beautiful weekend, isn't it?"
"Maybe," Pierre sighed, as he watched her walk into the kitchen, then sat on the sofa. "Actually it's a better start of a weekend than I've had in the past."
"What do you mean by that?" She inquired politely as she sauntered into the living room carrying a bottle of wine with champagne glasses.
"We'll get to me later," Pierre countered, grinning. "Let's talk about you. So what do you do for a living."
"Medical receptionist, you?"
"I'm the head of the technical division Burke and Burke Advertising Company."
"Do you like it?"
"I love it. Dreamed of doing it since I was a child."
"Doing it?"
"No, illustrating," he looked surprised.
"I just wanted to see how you would react."

31

She was smiling mischievously. "Welcome to Stonehenge."
"Thank you."
They smiled at each other, drank.

They talked for hours, sipping on wine and enjoying the music, sometimes reminiscing back on things they enjoyed in the past. Sandra enjoyed herself completely. The wine seemed to calm her nervousness, reassuring her control of the conversation.
Here is a guy who is letting her take control, doesn't mind answering her and telling her how he feels from the heart, being a total gentleman and not trying to push up on her on their first so-called date. This she decided, she could get with.

"Well, it's getting late," observed Pierre, glancing at his watch. "I enjoyed your company, the wine, and the music. I only wish to make it up to you by taking you out, maybe next week, if I'm not being too direct."
"No, you're not. I was expecting you to ask," she reassured him. "I enjoyed this as much as much as you did."
"Thanks, " he replied.
"It only gets better," she stated invitingly, gazing into his eyes.
Taking her other arm he pulled her close, leaned forward and gently kissed her on the cheek. Her mind drifted as she tried to control herself, she felt dizzy. Damn, he's good!
"Call me," she purred as she watched him leave.

****

This is not how she had imagined their first conversation would be. He was like a different person, unlike the ones she used to talk. There was lots of warmth in him. But she couldn't figure out that wall that he held intentionally between them. He took her up on her offer. Maybe he was just scaling the wall. Now she found herself climbing this wall, trying to reach him. She found this wonderful person. It was obvious she was sexually attracted to him. But something was different. She didn't know where he was coming from or what he was searching for. She didn't understand him or herself. Usually she would make her move. He probably was trying to convince himself. He was so debonair. Any other many would have tried to move on her the first night. She knew damn well she wanted him, and maybe he she, so why didn't he try? So many thoughts raced through her mind that she wanted solved, quickly. But she couldn't rid Herself of the longing that overwhelmed her every time she thought of him, pictured him in her mind, remembering his voice, his touch, his kiss. She went upstairs, changed into Her silk chemise, then lay in bed, recollecting the night. This man is the one I have been dreaming of, she thought as she drifted off to sleep, content with herself for being so lucky.

5

PIERRE

That second Saturday in April, Pierre had dinner that evening with Sandra at Cafe' de la Place, an French restaurant that was constructed several hundred feet in the air that slowly revolved, offering diners with a spectacular view of Atlanta's skyline. The weather was holding well this year. The full moon casted an ominous glow, making the sky looks as if it was from a painter's canvas. After checking their coats and being shown to the table, Sandra went to the powder room, while Pierre ordered drinks. When she returned, Pierre was staring out the window, taking in the view while casually sipping on white wine.

"So what's a handsome gentleman like yourself doing living by yourself?" Sandra asked questionly as Pierre pulled her chair for her, made sure she was comfortable, then sat down across from her.

Pierre looked at Sandra and took a deep breath. "Things happened to me in the past that I haven't gotten over completely."

"What things? Sandra asked, her beautiful expressive eyes filled with concern for him.

"It's a long story."

"Tell me if it doesn't bother you," Sandra suggested. "We have time."

So Pierre told her, starting with the accident outside his in-laws place and leaving out nothing till he moved to Stonehenge.

When he finished, he was feeling for them, but he was immensely relieved that he could talk to someone that somewhat cared about how he felt.

The waiter arrived with the food and served them, and before leaving, inquired if they need anything just raise their hand. As the waiter turned away, Sandra looked into Pierre eyes and leaned forward, giving him her total attention.

"I know how you feel and I'm your friend, we can work this out together," she said, gazing into his eyes. "Just take it slow."

"I am," Pierre said shyly. "Starting now"

They enjoyed their meal completely, talking without pause all evening, speaking with urgency. As they drove to his apartment, she liked him more with each new thing she learned about him. She had begun to think they might go to bed together, tonight. By the time they arrived at his place she knew they would. Pierre wasn't pushing her. For that matter she wasn't either. They were simply driven by natural forces, like a rush of mountain water downstream. Like calm before the storm. On an instinctual level, the booth realized they were in need of each other, physically, mentally, and emotionally and that whatever happened between them would be right and good.

After they took off their shoes and Pierre made a small fire and brought her a glass of wine, he gave her a nickel tour of his place.

"Who decorated the place? Did you hire an interior decorator?"

"No, I think a decorator is too impersonal with a lot of things that are not your taste but theirs. I did this myself."

"You did! This is beautiful! How did you do it?"

"Well, when I was young, I looked forward to having better things, then, when I had the money, I didn't want to have strange furnishing. I wanted to do it myself. Kim and I decorated our first place. The job became a hobby for her and I spent as much time on it as I did on my drawings. We went furniture shopping all over from Birmingham, AL to Miami, FL, from flea markets to the most expensive stores. We had a good time. And when she died......I couldn't get over the loss if I stayed in a place that was full of memories of her and my son. For two to three years I was a wreck cause every object in the house reminded me of them. Finally I took a few mementos, a couple of things I'd remember them by, moved out, after my lease expired, bought this townhouse and started decorating all over."

"Your place is beautiful."
"Thanks."

As the hours drifted, they talked as if they were old friends. She never was sure who initiated the first kiss. He may have leaned toward her, or perhaps tilted toward him. But it was inevitable.

"We hardly know each other," she said.
"Is that the way you feel?"
"No."
"Me neither."
"I know you so well, seem like ages, yet it's only been one week, what do you think?"
"Not too fast for me."
"Not to fast at all," she agreed.
"Sure?"
"Positive."
"You're beautiful."
"Love me."

Their lips met softly, briefly. Then again, and a third time. And then he began planting small kisses all over her face; on her forehead, on her eyes, on her cheeks, on her nose, the corners of her mouth, her chin. He kissed her ears, her eyes again, and left a chain of kisses along her neck, and when at last returned to her mouth he kissed her more deeply than before. And she responded at once, opening her mouth to him, nibbling, licking, pushing her tongue between his lips, taking his tongue into her mouth. His hand moved slowly over her, testing the firmness and resilience of her, and she touched him too, gently squeezing his shoulders, his arms, the hard muscles of his back. Nothing felt better to her than he felt at that moment.

As if drifting in a dream, they left the living room, and went to the bedroom. He touched a small Japanese touch lamp that stood on the bedside dim and turned down the sheets.

During the minute he was away from her, he was unsure about this. But when she came behind him and hugged him tentatively, he found that he was sure, turned and pressed against her once more. He picked her up as if she were a child. She clung to him. She saw a longing and a need in his light brown eyes, a powerful wanting that was only partly sex and she knew the same need to be loved and valued must be in her eyes for him to see. He carried her to bed, put her down, and urged her to lie back. Without haste, with breathless anticipation that lit his face, he undressed her.

He lowered his face to hers. As they kissed, she slid a hand between his legs, then squeezed and stroked him slowly. She felt wanton, shameless, insatiable. As he entered her, she let her hands travel over his muscular body, along his lean flanks.

"You're so sweet," she moaned.

He began the sweet music of lovemaking. For a long time, they forgot that time existed, and they explored the delicious, silken surfaces of love, and it seemed to them, in those morning hours, that they would love forever.

WANTING EYES

Sandra stayed the night with Pierre and she realized that she forgotten how pleasant it could be to share a bed with someone you truly deeply cared for; She'd had other men in bed and had stayed overnight with a few, but not one of those other lovers had made her feel warm and constant, just by the sheer fact of their presence. Like Pierre with Sandra, sex was a delightful bonus, but it wasn't the main reason she wanted to be there beside him. He was an excellent lover, smooth eager to please and uninhibited in the pursuit of giving her pleasure-but he was also a person, a person worth knowing, not stamped out of any mold, different, and it was his unique personality, heart and soul that made sharing his bed a very special privilege. She realized it wasn't really sex that he needed from her. What he needed was merely to be close, to hold her, to touch her, to obtain comfort from her. That was something she needed too; a deep soothing display of affection; reassurance. But she had always been under the impression that such innocent affection, utterly unassociated with sex was exclusively a woman's need. She was somewhat surprised to find Pierre seeking that sort of compassion and tenderness from her. Now as she held Pierre and was held by him, she realized, more than before, that she had been missing a great deal in life. It was nice knowing someone like him was there. A man with whom she could share more than just good times. For a while she lay there, listening to his breathing she drifted off to sleep.

****

The next morning they woke and made love in the shower. It was better than the previous night because they were familiar with each others bodies and moves. They clung to each other passionately, locked in a heavenly embrace of love. Thoroughly spent and satisfied they showered, finished cleaning and toweling each other, and went into the bedroom.

"Do you have anything for me to wear?" She asked.

"You should find something in this dresser over here," he said, pointing to the dresser closest to him against the wall.

She changed into his boxers and one of his sweatshirts she found in the drawer. Putting his house slippers on, she kissed him on the forehead then headed for the kitchen, leaving him sitting on the bed with a satisfied look on his face.

Lost in thought, Pierre forgot about Sandra till he smelled the aroma of food cooking in the kitchen. He slipped into his lounge pants, then went to the kitchen to find food prepared and on the table for him. She was making a plate for herself when he came up behind her and hugged her. Kissing her on the back of her head, he went and sat down at the table and looked at the spread before him, approvingly. He had already started eating when she stopped him and took his hand in hers.

"You were wonderful last night."

"Thank you. You were beautiful too, but it felt strange."

"What do you mean?"

"Well, it felt strange because it had been a long time since I made love to someone besides my wife. I felt as if I was cheating."

He stared at her, but she knew he could not see her. His mind was elsewhere, lost in pleasant memories of his past. There was a long silence. Sandra broke it.

"Good things are not to be forgotten," she said quietly. "And you didn't do anything she wouldn't want you to do now that

39

she's gone. I wish I could take our pain away, but, in time to-gether we'll make it. Let's not rush anything. When the time is right, and you find what you're searching for, you'll know."

He said nothing for a while. She stole a glance at him from under her eyelashes, but could read nothing there.

Slowly his eyes refocused on her. "Thank you for being here, and most of all, for trying to understand me," he said with a warm smile on his face.

In spite of herself, she smiled. She thought she had reached him slowly at first, until her intentions were known. But for now her biggest task, she thought, would be doing everything in her power to replace the love he once had. Now as she watched him eat his food, she realized his pain is great but could be eased if he found what he was looking for. And she was determined to make sure his search would end with her in his arms.

MARCUS

Marcus unlocked the door to his studio and went in, without turning on the lights, and locked the door behind him. Leaning against the door, he sighed loudly. Things just weren't going right for him.

That night, after spending the evening at the Sandcastle, a local club that featured live jazz bands that performed on Saturdays, he ran into Monique with one of her men, while taking pictures to promote the band and club. Just watching them enjoy themselves made him realize how much he loved her. But he wasn't sure it was love or just jealously stemmed from her being with someone instead of him. Seeing her laughing, drinking, and enjoying the company of her male companion stirred feelings in him he never knew he had. She was a beautiful, dark skin sister with long black hair, a face with high cheekbones and deep black almond eyes. Body that was voluptuous and full; nice firm breasts and a slim stomach that was tight ever since she ran track in college. Firm, muscular thighs and big calves that a perfectly round ass sat on. He loved every minute of their lovemaking as she was insatiable to please. They were alike, both wanted to be free without the restrictions of a relationship. But now, seeing her with another made him feel strange.

They left about two-thirty. He watched them leave. Now feeling worried cause he knew what he'd be doing about this time, he busied himself around the club, finished the shoot, then sat at the bar and had a couple of drinks. Feeling rambunctious and a little horny, he calls Lisa and lets her know he is spending the night with her. He packed his camera and equipment in his car and left, knowing full well he was gonna get laid. It was a booty call. She knew too, as she waited for him, watching late night shows. Maybe it was the heat of the moment, caught up in the passion of climaxing as he sexed her, he made one of biggest mistakes he had ever made; He called out another female name in the height of ecstasy.

Disgusted, Lisa pushed him off and slapped him. An argument ensued, ending with him begging and pleading at her apartment door. He left, knowing she wouldn't forgive him for that. She was a good woman, he just took too many things for granted, and love was one of them.

Going upstairs to his studio-style apartment that was right above his studio, he labored on each step. Exhausted, he fell back on his bed, rolled over and tapped the button on his answering machine. It spoke, with an electronic voice, telling him how many messages he had, then rewinding and ending with a beep, started playing messages. He stared at the ceiling listening to them. None of them were from Monique, just clientele. He knew she had seen him, she winked at him as he walked around, taking pictures of couples having a good time. He picked up the phone and press the speed dial, laid back and waited for it to ring. After the first ring, he hung up. He was the one that wanted this type of relationship and now he's the one that's breaking first. Thoughts raced in his mind as he contemplated

42

having a normal relationship with Monique. Shaking his head, he changed his mind at the mere thought of being committed. He walked over to his full length mirror and watched himself, as he took off his jewelry and laid it on the dresser, then stripped out of his clothes. Walking to the bathroom, he took a shower and changed into his silk pullovers. Feeling refreshed but tired, he lay across his bed and thought about the night as he drifted off to sleep.

****

He awoke to his phone ringing off the hook. Groggily he stretched out, picked it up, and pressed the receive button.

"Yeah?"

"Yeah? Is that the way to answer your phone? Wake yo ass up!"

Pierre.

"What's up man? Why are you up so early? What time is it?" Marcus asked.

"I'm not up early, its two o'clock. Look, when you get up, don't forget the playoffs are on tonight at seven. We're watching it over Rob's this time, bet?"

"Bet."

"How was the shoot last night?"

"Great, but afterwards I caught a case with Lisa."

"What did you do this time?"

"Long story. Anyway, what's up with you? We were supposed to do this shoot together, remember?"

"I had a date."

"What!"

"Look, we'll talk later. I gotta make a few runs and I'll see you at Rob's okay? You gettin up?"

"Yeah, Dominique is coming over at five. I'm not bringing her though. She's gonna chill here."

"Boy, you need to stop. I holla."

"Peace."

Marcus laid bed for a minute, collecting his thoughts, then reached over and grabbed his stereo remote off the night stand. Turning his stereo off he got up, walked to the edge of the loft that looked out over his apartment and sighed. He had some cleaning to do before Dominique comes over. Though his apartment was slightly dirty, it was nice. Everything was open, spacious, comfortable, and affordable since his studio was below. He liked the layout of his apartment. The walls were the color of reddish brown. It was such a soothing tone that it immediately set the mood when you walked into the room. His bedroom was on a split level loft that a stairway led to. His king size bed was very large but surprisingly comfortable, with shades of warm browns and rusts, and gold; lots of large cushy pillows and small throw pillows that you could just sink into and sleep for hours, was against the far wall under a large window that had a beautiful view of the park and Atlanta's skyline in the far distance amongst the trees. The night stands, made of beautiful pickled wood, stood on each side of the bed with two wooden African carved lamps on them. The dresser stood against the wall next to his full length mirror. His small dresser that his stereo sat on was on the opposite wall. Downstairs his private bar, stocked with his favorite liquors, stood against the wall near the stairway that led to his studio. The L-shaped couch with recliner was Marcus's favorite spot, with all its pillows and comfort, and served as a bed for him sometimes on many a night when he was just too tired to go upstairs to the loft, stood facing the fireplace against the east wall. His love seat sat adjacent to it facing towards the large window on the south wall. The wide screen TV and entertainment system sat next to the fireplace with his speakers positioned carefully around the apartment so you could hear the music perfectly. The surround sound speakers stood on each side of the couch and gave excellent theatrical sounds when he watched movies. The kitchen was complete with a breakfast bar and wine storage compartment. Under the bedroom loft, his refrigerator and a freezer stood against the wall across from the kitchen. His bathroom had full bath and shower with a door separating it from the lavatory. Next to the bathroom was his walk-in closet.

WANTING EYES

****

Within the hour, he had finished cleaning the place. Exhausted, he went to the refrigerator, grabbed a beer and sipped it, gazing out the window. Satisfied, he went to pick the clothes he was going to wear, and run water in the shower. He was pleased with himself and took pride in wearing his clothes, to sporting his jewelry. Everywhere he went was opportunity to meet ladies, and he did not want to be caught slipping. He finished his shower and carefully took his time in oiling his body and putting cologne on. Gazing in the mirror with nothing but his silk pullovers on, he smiled at his appearance. He put on his Jordache boxer briefs. Carefully placing talc powder on his chest to smell nice, he donned his white Tom Hilfiger shirt, and his black Walter Davoucci overalls. Lotioning his feet, he placed on his Gucci socks and his Boss boots. He stood, looking at his self in the full length mirror as he placed on his jewelry. He posed in the mirror. *Damn I look good*! He walked away watching himself as the intercom beeped. He went down to the living room to the monitor that was flashing on the wall near the bar, pressed it and fixed himself a drink.

"Who's this?"
"You know who this is, buzz me up."

Dominique.

"You're early," he said.
"I wanted to spend a little time with you before you hang with the boys, is that okay with you?"
"Yeah, yeah I likes that," he replied as he buzzed her up, then stood at the top of the stairway, waiting for her to come up.

46

"How's my baby been?" He asked, as he hugged her and gave her a kiss.

"Fine, work made me tired, but I'm glad it's the weekend."
"You smell nice and look good."
"Thank you."
"You sure you're just going to watch a game with the boys?"
"Yeah, baby, you know me."
"Yeah, you never know when business will find you."
"True that. Now, you get comfortable, and I'll put on some jazz and massage you till I have to go."
"Now that sounds nice."

She went in, placed her overnight bag in the bedroom, changed out of her clothes and showered. Putting on his silk pullovers and one of his T-shirts, went and laid on the living room couch beside him as he started to massage her with the smoothness of being massaged over the years.

They talked, making small talk for the sake of it, passing time. She loved the way he gave her attention, and wanted him to give himself to her completely. But not living together made it difficult to monopolize his time. But she'll change that soon.

Checking his watch, he looked at her with pouted lips.

"Gotta run," he said.
"I know."
"I'll be back as soon as it's over. Got the number to his place right?"
"Yeah."
"Okay."
"I'll have a surprise for you when you return," she added seductively.
"I'll be ready," he said, kissing her on the forehead.

He arrived at Rob's place just as Pierre pulled up. They parked their cars, got out, and gave each other a pound as they walked up to the door. Rob's wife Marie, met them at the door and led them to the family room where Rob and his son Christian, were already watching the pre-game show. They sat down as she went into the kitchen and brought them beers.

"What's up?" Rob prompted. "Ready for the Magic to put the Bulls away?"

"It's not gonna be that easy," Marcus answered, shaking his head.

"Why?"

"Cause his Airiness is back!" proclaimed Pierre, leaning as if he was dunking in an imaginary hoop.

"This series will go seven," Marcus interjected.

""We'll see," muttered Rob.

Marie came in with the snacks and set them on the coffee table.

"Okay, the beer is in the fridge, and you have snacks. Is there anything else you need before Christian and I go to the mall?"

"Nothing," replied Marcus.

"Thanks, we're good," Pierre answered.

"Yeah, thanks honey, " Rob whispered as he got up, hugged and kissed his wife, and patted his son on the head. "I'll make sure they leave the family room in one piece, when their beloved Bulls lose. You need some money?"

"No, this is mom's treat," She explained. "Enjoy the game."

He walked her to the door, then to the car, and watched them leave. Running back into the house, he grabbed the remote and turned the TV down.

"Okay, what's really goin on? Marcus told me you had a date, what's the 411?" asked Rob.

"Yeah, drop it on us, we want to know everything," added Marcus.

"Aw ight, I met this female that lives in the building, you know, anyway we went out," Pierre said.

Marcus and Rob looked at each other, then shot him a surprised look.

"And that was it?", said Marcus, spurring him on.

"No, and I hit it," replied Pierre, nonchalantly as if it was an everyday happening.

"The first night!" Stated Rob, eyes wide. "You don't waste any time!"

"Yesss!" Marcus interjected, pumping his fist. "He hasn't lost his touch."

"It wasn't like I meant to, it just happened," added Pierre.

"Yeah, that does happen, I do it all the time," taunted Marcus jokingly. "I meet a female, we talk, I trip and fall off into the pussy and say 'I'm sorry babe, it just happened'"

They all laughed except Pierre.

"No, I mean we just happened to need each other," suggested Pierre.

"I think one needed it more, " continued Marcus laughing.

They laughed until Pierre shot them a serious look.

Then Pierre told them, starting with dinner and leaving nothing out until they ended at his place.

"So she's getting over a divorce," Rob inquired.

"Yeah."

"Bad move," stated Marcus, shaking his head.

"Why?"

Marcus explained. "Some women go through a lot of changes with a man they love and he doesn't act right. And it heightens to the point that they divorce with her having mixed emotions. So when they meet someone, they don't want to go through the same thing, so they're very skeptical, emotional, and some are possessive and jealous if the divorce was over another woman. Gotta be careful."

"Were gonna take it slow."

"Yeah, looks like you've started on a slow tip."

They laughed and drank, while Pierre smiled.

"Well, since we're on the point of females," Rob declared. "Let me tell you about this honey at work that's pushing up on me."

"Man, you think a woman wants you if she smiles at you," teased Marcus, trying hold his laughter in.

"Yo, yo, the games on," said Pierre, reaching for the remote and turning the volume up. "We'll finish the subject after the game."

50

****

To Rob's disappointment, the Bulls trounced the Magic 113 - 89. They finished watching the game, waited to see who was picked for Player of the Game, then carried their drinks and snacks into the den to play pool.

"I'm gonna play till I lose," stated Marcus, racking the balls. "I don't want to keep Dominique waiting."

"That's cool," replied Rob.

"What's up with the female you have to tell us about?" asked Pierre, tapping Marcus.

"Yeah, whatsupwitdat?" Marcus added.

So Rob told them about how at work this young intern named Shelly is pushing up on him from sly suggestive remarks to asking him over to her place. When he finished, he asked them for their advice.

"There is nothing to think about," suggested Pierre, after he broke the rack. "Your happily married and have a beautiful son."

"I'd hit it," stated Marcus smiling, walking around the table, picking a shot. "Just think of it as keeping your marriage from being dull."

"That's bullshit!" Pierre countered. "Outside relations always lead somewhere and it is bad. Do you love your wife."

"Dearly," answered Rob.

"Then I wouldn't do it."

"If you love your wife you'd hit it," repeated Marcus, wincing as he missed a close shot.

"You'll hit anything that moves," teased Pierre, squaring up for a shot. "Every time you come to my house my goldfish stop swimming."

51

They all laughed as Marcus smiled.

"It's your choice," continued Pierre, suddenly turning serious. "But if it was me I wouldn't do it."

"Hit it," instructed Marcus, patting Rob on the back. "It's excitement for he marriage, a change you'll see."

They finished playing, then Marcus played Rob. Afterwards he walked them outside to their cars.

"Well," Pierre sighed. "You asked for our opinions and we gave it. But you know, opinions are like assholes, everyone has one."

He gave him a pound and got in his car. Rob turned and looked at Marcus. Marcus grinned and shrugged. "I'd hit it."

Rob pushed him away, smiled and gave him a pound, then watched them as they drove away.

****

    That night as he laid in bed next to Marie snuggled up to him, he thought of everything that was said that evening. He loved his wife dearly and his son, but he felt as if he was missing out on something. When he was single, he had to practically hunt women down. Now married, responsible, mature, and with a son, women are constantly flirting with him, as if to make marriage hard enough. He didn't understand it. It seemed when you get married, women like it more when you are someone else's. Marcus and him been out many times, and every time opportunity knocked. Marie and him have a wonderful relationship. They have wonderful talk, not afraid to speak about what ambitions they have, or what pressing issues they have that bothers them. They have sex often, if not a lot, and it had been wonderful. Now he's starting to think that boredom has settled in. He knew when his wife wanted him and all the signs. Now craving for something different, he decided that if and when it happened, he wasn't going to be the one who initiated. She would have to pursue him. Content with the rising lust and excitement of the unexplored, he went to sleep.

PIERRE

Despite the hour, Pierre walked over to Sandra's apartment. Using the keys she gave him, he opened the door and was surprised to see Sandra was up waiting for him.

"What took you so long to come home?" Sandra demanded as he came through the door. "I thought you just went over Rob's for the game?"

"We did watch the game," he explained. "But afterwards we shot some pool and talked, why?"

"Who's we?"

"Rob, Marcus and I. What's wrong?"

"Nothing, I was just worried. You should have called."

"Called! You knew where I was, hangin with the boys, and if I would have journeyed elsewhere I would have called!"

"I don't like you hanging with them!" Sandra snapped. "I think they're bad influence!"

They argued back and forth. Over him drinking, to his friends, to him staying late. Pierre was surprised, but tried to understand her way of thinking, but it was impossible. It was

just like everything changed after the intimate night, that wonderful night they spent together. She practically thought he was
hers to have. Without consent.

Not wanting to blow things out of proportion, he apologized
before she went with him over to his place. Going into the bedroom, he changed and took a shower, while she laid on the bed,
watching him. When he came out she asked to stay with him.
He declined.

"I think I want to be alone tonight," he answered. "Besides,
the drinks have me slightly drunk and I have a headache."
"You need some aspirin," she suggested. "Get in the bed and
I'll bring you some."

Rising up off the bed, she went into the bathroom. Leaving
the room, she went to the kitchen. She asked him when she
brought him some aspirin if she could get him anything else before he went to sleep. She was standing by the bed. He reached
up and took her hand in his.

"Thank you, and I'm sorry. I'll try to do better," he said
apologetically.

His eyes were so compelling that she had to pull away. What
she really wanted to do was to sit down on the bed and put her
arm around him. To kiss him. To make love to him. But she
didn't.

All he needed to do was to pull ever so gently on her hand
and she would have came to him. But he didn't. She could tell
he wanted to. But he didn't. Somehow it was important to him
that they come on a level of understanding without using sex as
a cure for every argument they had. She also understood that the
next time they made love when it happens, if it happens, he
wanted to make the first move. She didn't sleep well that night.

All she could think about was being with him, making love to him. Sometimes it seemed impossible, the idea of it. So forbidden and different, not only for her, but she knew for him as well. Other times the idea of not making love to him was impossible. Sometimes sex seemed so immediate, so natural for her. Just another bodily function. She felt that she knew him so well that it would only be an extension of what they already had.

Everybody did it. All the time. Monique always said that everybody fucked. Everybody cheated on their spouses. If you suspected people were fucking, they were surely fucking. Everyone in Atlanta fucked. In fact she was a perfect example. Before she met Pierre, she did it to a married man and enjoyed it. But somehow with Pierre, she wasn't about to reduce it to that. Anything that happened with him will have to be from the heart than just sex. That sounded corny, but it was true. He couldn't be just another lay. Certainly he was a seasoned lover, she found that out from their first encounter and smiled when she remembered. But now she had to make him all hers. Content with her reasoning, she drifted off to sleep.

MARCUS

When Marcus returned that evening, Dominique had just gotten out of the shower. She had on one of his robes, which she found in the closet that he claimed he didn't know he had.

"I've been waiting for you," she purred, walking towards him as her robe fell to the floor, allowing him to gaze at her beauty.

She had one of the most beautiful bodies he had ever seen. Brown sugar. A light brown tush to match her hair, and her breasts sprang out as soon as the robe fell. And she wasn't shy. She started undressing Marcus, unbuttoning his overalls and pulling up his shirt. When he pulled off his shirt, she ran her hands over his belly and his crotch and leaned her face against his stomach. As she pulled down his boxer briefs, he touched her head downward and with that encouragement she did what she wanted to do. He let her for a while and then picking her up, carried her to bed.

They made love, and when it was over, she buried her face in his neck with her arms around him and sighed contentedly.

"Isn't this nice?" Dominique sighed as she played with his chest hairs.

"Yeah, it was wonderful," Marcus replied.

"No, I mean this, you and I, together right now?"

"What are you talking about?"

Dominique looked up into Marcus's eyes, then back down to her moving hand.

"I mean, we've been together for seven months and I'm tried of sleeping over, a weekend here and there. And trying to catch up with you. I know you're busy, but what I really want to say is I want to move in with you. I really want to be here for you, baby. What do you think?"

"I think we should get some rest and we'll talk this over seriously tomorrow, okay?"

He played in her hair and kissed her on her forehead. She smiled, nodded and closed her eyes. She rested while Marcus laid awake, thinking about it.

He wanted the feeling, but the attachment he felt he could do without. He had others lovers and wanted to spread his attention evenly to all of them. But mostly what kept him from commitment was Monique. They were so alike and even though they have that understanding, he was strangely possessive towards her. He wanted to be with her, but he didn't want to make it happen. Somehow if it happened it had to be both of them in agreement. As he thought, his mind wandered till he fell asleep.

10

ROB

For nearly two weeks, Rob worked the mid shift at the hospital. It was fairly easy, considering the job he did. In the morning he had to assess the patients' condition by taking their temperature, blood pressure, pulse and recording the process. Afterwards any medications, injections or dressings that needed changing was completed. If a patient was due for surgery, he would have them prepped. Finally, after the priorities have been completed he would assist them with their personal needs. He was a good worker, patient and diligent in his efforts while keeping a very favorable line of communication with all patients. They felt like one of the family when he was there and looked forward to talking with him when he was on shift.

He had avoided her for a while, fearing contact would put him in a compromising position. But as he left the main office, he almost knew it was inevitable. He was told that Shelley was going to join his staff and for one week, he was suppose to take her and show her his rounds, introduce her to his patients, because he was going to take a more supervisory role on the shift.

He welcomed the promotion cause he could spend more time at home, and didn't have to spend too much time on his feet except for making rounds, checking his patients' progress. But working with Shelley for a week, boy! Would he need help. The woman was fine!

She was short with a mulatto complexion, light hazel eyes and straight black hair that she wore shoulder length, with long layers scissored on an angle from her cheekbones to ends around her face. A shapely figure that Rob had seen ever grace a uniform. Firm, muscular calves that showed from beneath her uniform that she spends some of her off-duty time in a gym. A sexy voice that gained your attention when she spoke.

Now, as the first day of them working together was ending he wished to relieve himself of her presence so she wouldn't have the opportunity to address him and he, given that temptation of seduction that he knew he wouldn't turn down.

"Well, on more patient before the swing shift comes in," Rob explained as they walked down the corridor. "You can go ahead and sign out if you want to. Mr. Ross is pretty grumpy, especially with the medication he's on."

"I was thinking that I'll help you with him, then we'll sign out together and go somewhere and have a drink," she suggested, with an innocent look on her face. "Besides, I need a ride home if that's okay, I mean if your wife wouldn't mind."

Rob shot her a surprised look.

"What are you saying?"

"I'm saying you've been avoiding me purposely. You scared of me?"

"I'm not scared of you. I'm just trying to keep this on a professional level."

"I am being professional," she whispered in his ear. "I'm containing myself from not taking you into one of these empty rooms and raping you."

"Why me?"

"Why not? Your handsome, intelligent, mature, and you turn me on. Besides, it looks like you want me but you're afraid to make the advance. Don't worry, I won't tell your wife if that's what you think. Call her and tell her you'll be late," she insisted. "Hospitals have emergencies, you know."

WANTING EYES

They finished their rounds thirty minutes early. She went to change clothes, while he finished up some paperwork in his office. Meeting her in the parking lot, the look on his face would have told her he wanted her, but it was hid by the shadow of the night. She was fine! She had finally shed her saintly uniform and the effect was a transformation. He had been so used to her wearing her uniform around that he was taken back by her wearing civilian clothes. Her clothes were conservative and in good taste, enhancing her bodies' strong points. Her breasts were full and her waist was very small. Her buttocks was nice and well-rounded with shapely curved hips. With her loafers, she stepped with more grace and her walk was breathtaking. The transformation from an angel of mercy to a woman was complete.

Now, as he gazed at her walking nonchalantly towards his car, he knew he had to hit it, if only once. He hurried to unlock his car and let her in. Driving out of the parking lot, they headed for the expressway going towards downtown, where she knew of a nice place they could be together, but not seen. The sky was clear and dark, like blue velvet besetted with many small diamonds clustered around on it, twinkling as he drove. He contemplated just turning her down and taking her home. But his passion and lust of desire overcame him thinking clearly.

They parked and went into the Blue Note, a nice jazz club that featured up and coming talents in it. Seated where it was easy to watch incoming traffic, He prayed that Marcus would not be prowling tonight. He'd rather tell them than have Marcus trip on him, then call Pierre and brag how he took his advice.

He ordered drinks while Shelley watched him.

"Don't be nervous," she reassured him. "If you don't want to go through with this, I understand."

"I want to," he explained. "But it just feels weird to be out with someone other than my wife."

"Well, let me do something to relax you," she replied, as she slipped her hand under the table and stroked him slowly.

They made small talk and drank until the tension and desire built up till he couldn't take it. Paying for the drinks and leaving a tip, they went to the car and drove off.

Giving directions, she teased him on the way there, blowing and lightly flickering her tongue in his ear, while rubbing his crotch.

WANTING EYES

They made it to her apartment complex safe. Hurrying inside, they got in the elevator just as the doors closed. She pressed against him as they kissed, hands wandering and grabbing with wanton desire. Her tongue penetrated his lips hungrily, searching. They untangled each other as the elevator stopped with a ring and the doors sprung open invitingly.

They hurried to her apartment. She unlocked the door and paused, teasing him, her smile lingered long enough as her tongue slid across her lips. He came forward and grabbed her in his arms. His kiss was hungry, penetrating. She ran her hands down his back and grabbed his buttocks, then moved her fingers back up his spine, feeling the cords of muscles at her fingertips. He was physically strong, no doubt about that. It was clear he worked out with weights regularly.

"Your strong," she whispered against his cheek, her hands stroking his chest.

"Let me show you how strong I am."

She pulled back a few inches. They undressed each other slowly, enjoying unveiling their bodies. Dressed in panties, she picked up his clothes and folded them on a chair. She turned to see him silhouetted in the dim light, then smiled as she glanced down to see the bulge growing in his boxers.

"Take off your boxers," she asked.

With a touch of male pride in his organ, he slipped off his boxers. A long, hard penis emerged like a sword from a sheath.

Following his lead, she turned around, spread her legs slightly, and bent down, arching her back as she pulled her panties down to her knees. Looking back at him seductively, she slowly straightened up and let her panties fall to her feet.

Before she could step out of them he came to her, his arms around her waist, his long penis pressed hot and hard against her buttocks as he pulled her to him and spun her around slowly.

They stood pressed hard to each other, kissing again as his hands grabbed her buttocks tightly and ground her against his crotch. He picked her up with a quick scoop, while her legs curled gently around him. He was showing off his strength, as he kissed her, then he bent to place her on the bed.

He kissed her breasts, nibbling carefully at the hard nipples. Then he kissed his way back up around her neck and ears. Already knowing that he wanted her and she was as excited as he, she gripped his sex gently in her long fingers and let him inside her.

He groaned as he entered her. Her sex was so wet and hot that he couldn't contain himself. Caught up in lust, he stroked faster, while she squirmed with ecstasy and arched her back, trying to take all of him inside her deeply. At last he succumbed to his climax. She climaxed with him, sighing at the ecstasy he gave her. When it was over, they laid in each others arms, breathless and satisfied.

WANTING EYES

****

They made love three more times before he showered and left her. All three times were more pleasurable than the first, as they talked and made love and talked, as though the two forms of pleasures went hand in glove.

He left her at three in the morning. She lay nude in bed and looked beautiful, showing off her body as if to tempt him as he blew her a kiss good-bye.

He finally returned home, tired and sleepy. Carefully slipping into the house, he quickly undressed and got into bed, lingering only for a moment in thought as he fell asleep, not aware that Marie was just lying, lightly sleeping in bed, waiting for him to come home.

Next morning Rob awoke late, and slowly made his way to the kitchen where Marie had cooked breakfast for him. Glancing at her at the table where she was sitting down, reading the newspaper, he went to the refrigerator and helped himself to a glass of orange juice. Walking towards her, he kissed her on the head then sat across from her.

"Good morning honey," she said softly. "How'd last night go?"

"Busy," Rob explained. "I was leaving and we had a trauma patient come in emergency. He was going to be assigned to our wing so we stayed to assist.."

"We?"

"Yeah, Shelley and I."

"And it took till four in the morning, for this emergency?"

"Baby, you know how these things go-"

"Yes," she interrupted. "I know how these things go, but you should have called when you had time. I waited up for you!"

"I'm sorry."

"Yeah, you're sorry," she said flatly as she rose, made his plate and dropped it on the table in front of him.

"Here is your food honey, I gotta run."

"Where are you going?"

"I'm running some errands with Mom today so I should be home later. You'll pick up Christian from school, okay?"

"But I thought we were going to spend quality time today?" he argued as he rose, grabbed her by the arm and slid the other around her waist as he eased behind her.

"I waited up for you so we could," she stated, pulling his arms down. "But since an emergency took priority, I really don't feel like it right now. When I come back, we'll see okay?"

She pulled herself away and went into the bedroom. Coming back into the kitchen, she threw a black silk negligee at him.

"I was wearing this last night!" She snapped. "Remember this one you bought for me when we went on vacation to Tahiti?"

"I can't forget."

"Only on special occasions, right?"

"Right."

"But since that emergency had you tired last night and you fell asleep the minute you hit the bed, you didn't notice."

"But..."

"Later."

She left him standing there, watching as she grabbed her jacket and pursed and stormed out. He had mixed emotions so he was glad she left so he could think about things. Sighing he turned, sat down, looked at his breakfast and started to eat.

11

PIERRE

Today Pierre was in a hurry. His boss called early, asking him if he could make it to an important meeting. This was odd, because usually he would know when and where the weekly meetings would be held, and who would be in charge of the different accounts given to the company. He felt that it must be something very important that was going to happen and he was involved. Either good or bad he was very nervous. He was very good at his job, and the work that flowed from his department was highly commended by his peers and clients alike. But as always, a change in his normal routine made his heart flutter and hands sweat.

He showered and changed, taking his time to pick something not flashy, but of good tasted to wear. He donned is gray Hugo Boss suit, the lucky one he wears when he feels nervous and walked over to the mirror to adjust the fit. This has to be something good, he thought. Things were going wrong elsewhere.

He didn't imagine that Sandra was that jealous and dominating, but she was. From the calls at work to coming over unannounced was bothersome, but now she wanted to be with him every minute when he was not at work. She moved in temporarily, to see if we could take it to the next level, and it was working was except for the way she acted. And the way she embarrassed him. She was moody and through a scene she made publicly he found out she had a very quick temper.

They went to the East side cinema to watch "Sliver" starring Sharon Stone. They arrived early and she went to the ladies room to freshen her makeup. While waiting in the lobby, two attractive ladies came in and paid for the same movie. Seeing Pierre alone, they came over and made some small talk. Sandra came back out and seen it, her whole face changed. Coming to him, she pulled him away from them rudely, and they went to sit down early. An argument ensued that was brought under control with her apologizing.

Watching the credits roll while they settled down, the ladies came in and sat a seat away from Pierre. Slumping in his seat, he sat leaning toward Sandra, with his legs toward the ladies direction, at an angle. The movie started and it was good, but they never finished watching it. During the second love scene, Pierre started smiling cause he liked what he was watching, and the ladies giggled. Sandra assumed they were talking to Pierre, then looked and seen one of the ladies legs positioned towards him, jumped up in the theater and hollered, "Get your legs off my man, bitch!"

Thoroughly embarrassed, Pierre tried to calm her down, but to no avail. Apologizing to the women for her behavior, he left upset. They argued all the way home, ending with her begging and pleading. But his mind was made up. She wanted to stay over but he said it was best that they had some space. By the time Pierre opened the door to his place, the phone was ringing.

Sandra.

She was apologizing.

He told her that they'll talk tomorrow and hung up.

From that incident things worsen till it just wasn't good for both of them to have a relationship. After many long conversations about her past, she agreed reluctantly to just be good friends. They still have sex on occasions more need than want and she stayed over, but as far as seeing others, they both have free rein.

Pierre smiled as he adjusted his tie and checked his hair in the mirror. A nice aroma was coming from the kitchen. Sandra was cooking breakfast, but he wasn't going to be able to enjoy it.

"Who was that on the phone?" She inquired politely, as he came in the kitchen, grabbed a piece of toast, and opened the refrigerator.

"It was Harold Burke," he explained. "Son of my boss. He wants me to come in early for an important meeting."

"Why?"

"I dunno. Probably someone specifically asked for me to head an account that I don't know."

She came around the table and closed the refrigerator for him, her beautiful expressive eyes filled with concern for him. "Something wrong?"

"I don't think so. You working today?" he asked questionably.

"No, I thought that maybe we could talk about us today."
"It will have to be when I get back, I gotta run."

He kissed her on the cheek, picked up a glass of orange juice as he grabbed an extra piece of toast. She hurried with him to the door holding his briefcase as he checked himself in the mirror.

Kissing him, she gazed into his eyes. "I'll be here waiting on you."

****

Within an hour, Pierre was at the office, talking to his secretary, trying to find out what was happening. He couldn't find out anything, everything was normal at the office. He knew he was doing a good job at the office, no doubt about that. He just felt as if he was going into Burke's office with his pants down.

When Pierre finally went into Burke's office, he tried to "read" him, but couldn't figure out anything. As usual, Burke made him make them both drinks.

"Congratulations on the Copeland account!" Burke exclaimed, raising his glass to him.
"For what?" He inquired politely as he sipped his drink.
Burke explained. "Mr. Copeland loved the video presentation, and he wants to borrow you to show it to his shareholders before they start the campaign on the product."
Before Pierre could say anything, he held up his hand. "So take the day off cause this evening you will be on a flight to Miami. My secretary has your whole schedule, including your tickets. I'll see you in two weeks. My dad is proud of you and so am I."
"Thank you, sir," Pierre muttered. "What can I say-"
"Don't say anything," Burke continued. "Just represent us well down there, okay? The extra week in Miami is our way of saying thank you."

Pierre shook his hand, finished his drink and left, stopping by his secretary's office to let her know the good news and giving her time off. Leaving work, he cruised home to share his good news. Perhaps it was too soon to tell for sure, but he had the feeling that fate had given him a second chance at happiness.

WANTING EYES

****

Thirty minutes later, Pierre was back at his place, excitedly explaining what had happened at the office to Sandra. He hurried around the apartment, gathering up things he needed to take on the trip. As he came out of the bathroom with his shaving kit, Sandra stopped him.

"I really want to talk about us before you leave," she said flatly. "Could you sit down for a minute?"

"It's gonna have to wait," he suggested, dropping the kit in his suitcase. "The company car will be here soon."

"It's always either the job or your friends that comes between us!" She snapped. "When will we have our time?"

"We have had our time, remember?" He countered, turning to face her. "But something happened and our time was spent, arguing. I think this trip will help us. We need the time away from each other to sort things out."

She shot him a concerned look, as he turned and continued to pack.

"I've always been there for you, I've done everything for you." she said. "I've sat by the phone, night after night when you said you would call, cooked meals you've never showed up to eat."

"What do I have to do," she said. "To make you open your heart and take me in? I'm only asking, you see, it's not a rhetorical question. Tell me and I'll do it."

The final word ended in a sob; He turned and hugged her as she buried her head in his chest and wept as he stroked her hair.

At last she looked up and dried her eyes.

"I love you," she said.

His silence told her many things. Most importantly was she was not loved equally in return.

"I really like you and I care for you a lot," he pleaded. "But we both need time to think. I'm not pushing you away, I just want things to be right for us, okay?"

She nodded in agreement as he pulled her to him and hugged her. A car horn blared, interrupting their silence as they held each other.

"I gotta go," he whispered softly in her ear. "I'll call you when I get situated."

She sighed as they embraced, then helped him and the driver gather his bags and put them in the trunk.

"I hope this time make you realize how much I care for you," she stated, tears streaming down her cheeks, as she kissed him on the cheek.
"I know how you feel," he answered, as he hugged her tentatively. "But I guess it's me being insecure. We'll see in two weeks. Take care of yourself for me okay?"

She nodded as he got into the car, then watched him as they drove off. Something told her, a feeling, maybe her sixth sense that this would be the last time they'll be together.

WANTING EYES

****

Despite the hour, Pierre turned up at Rob's house, as Rob came out of the house, walking groggily towards the car, rubbing his eyes.

"Congratulations! Man, I knew you were due," he said, giving him a pound. "What's up?"

"Here's the keys to my place," Pierre instructed. "I need you to water the plants and feed the fish, cool?"

"Bet."

"I gotta go."

"Hold up," Rob insisted. "I have to drop something hot in your ear."

"You've got five minutes."

So Rob explained about what happened with Shelley, from the hospital and not leaving out anything till he sexed her. When he finished, Pierre was shaking his head.

"You know you done fucked up."

"How? She knows I'm married, and I'm completely honest with her. She doesn't care."

"She cares." Pierre explained. "Women always want to be with the man they sleep with and that is what breaks up families. My advice is you've hit it, enjoyed it from what you've told me, now squash it before it goes too far, okay?"

"I hear you."

"I know you hear me, but are you gonna do It.?"

"Yeah."

"Cool, I'll holla when I get back, peace."

Rob watched as Pierre rode off. He knew it wasn't right, but now he's hooked. The sex was wonderful and he felt at peace with her. I have to hit it again, at least one more time before I called it off and that's what I intend to do, he thought was he walked back into the house.

12

MARCUS

The delicatessen was crowded with more people than Marcus had imagined. Mainly cause it was after the noon hour lunch rush. Yet it was seemingly quiet so Marcus didn't mind meeting Monique there. It was her favorite lunch spot and he wanted everything to be right when he talked to her. He chose a table towards a corner that he could see across the deli and out the windows easily.

Sitting down, a waiter came up and asked for his order. Instructing what to bring, he also left instructions with the waiter that if someone came looking for him, to direct them to his table.

She returned, bringing his drink and inquired politely if he needed anything else just raise his hand. Marcus didn't even acknowledge her presence.. He just nodded as he continued to stare out the window, watching the traffic on the busy street. Time has come in his life to make a decision and he didn't feel up to it, as always.

Dominique implored him to let her move in and he gave in reluctantly. She was moving in next week. All he could think of is he can't have the comfort of his place to entertain women.

Lisa didn't want nothing to do with him anymore cause of that little incident, and he has feelings for Monique that he was surprised he had. He laughed, thinking about how Rob and Pierre would be shocked, seeing him just having a relationship with one woman. He swore he'd never settle and lived up to it, but now he felt different. Even more so, the weekend he spent with Dominique was wonderful, but felt so incomplete. They made love and afterwards, while she slept, he sat with his head in his hands, thinking. Raising up, he went to the kitchen and fixed him a glass of wine and stood, gazing out the living room window. He wasn't happy. He realized something was missing, and the void would not be filled till Monique was in his life, completely.

His thoughts were interrupted by a hug and a kiss on his cheek. Surprised, he rose and hugged Monique, inhaling her scent enhanced by her perfume. Pulling her chair out for her, she sat down, then sat down across from her, reaching to hold her hands.

"Want something to drink?" He inquired politely.
"I'll have what you're having," she replied, smiling at him. "What's up baby? You miss me?"
"Not really," he teased, as he waved the waiter over. "I was bored and I wanted to see how you was doing."
"I see you haven't changed." She said flatly, pulling her hands away, raising up to leave. "I don't want to waste your time."
"Just kidding baby," he pleaded as he rose and stopped her. "I missed you. How's things with you?
She returned to her seat as he sat down. "Things are going well, the beauty shops' business is up now more than usual, summer is around the corner. Why do you want to see me and talk? We usually talk afterwards."

He smiled.

"Something on your mind?"

"Yeah, but first I just want to enjoy your presence with me here."

She shot him a surprised look.

They continued to talk, speaking of nothing of major importance, from Pierre and Sandra's situation to things he has been doing.

"You're avoiding something, Marcus," she stated, looking directly into his eyes. "What's wrong?"

So Marcus told her how he felt about her, and how he is tired of the relationship they're currently having and how he wants her to be a part of his life. When he finished, Monique was staring at him warmly with a smile on her face.

"Marcus, I understand you completely, but I don't think you've had a change of heart. We'll see in time, but for now, let's enjoy us together, now."

They finished their drinks and left for his place. When they arrived, Marcus fixed them some wine as Monique made herself comfortable.

"Monique, I really feel this way," he continued, giving her a glass of wine. "And if I have to prove to you, my actions will represent my feelings for you."

She smiled as they tapped glasses, drank.

That afternoon, as sun shone, basking his living room with a warm glow, they made love on the floor, as the rays covered their bodies. It felt so right, so complete to Marcus, not just another lay. For once in his life he finally felt happy.

WANTING EYES

****

Lying on the living room floor, Marcus rested while Monique rose, went and showered, and changed clothes. By the time she finished, he was sleeping quietly in a ball of silk sheets on the floor. She knelt down beside him and watched him sleep, contemplating on waking him up. She decided not to. She tried to understand what he was asking for, but all she could think of was how peaceful he looked sleeping. She understood what he wanted, but didn't know what to say to him. It was the first time he had ever told how he really felt, from the heart, and it scared her. This is one change in him she hadn't expected, but it felt good knowing that he had more feeling for her than he claimed. But she wanted him to show her. For the first time in Monique's life she was content with what was about to happen. Kissing him lightly on the forehead, she rose and glanced at her watch. Even though it was late, even if he was hers to have, she had a lot of things to do before he entered her life, completely.

Smiling to herself, she quietly let herself out of his place.

13

PIERRE

Some time later that afternoon Pierre arrived at Atlanta International, one of the largest airports in the world. Everyone was hustling and running, catching flights or meeting someone. He felt so distant, but after he had checked in and had an hour before his flight left, the nervousness and anticipation of what the meeting held in Miami, led him to an airport bar. He sat down at the bar and order a gin and tonic before he found himself sitting next to a very beautiful flight attendant.

He gazed but tried not to stare at her, but couldn't help himself. She was beautiful and jazzy the way she sipped on a soda, casually talking to the bartender. Long, black, curly hair. Pretty, deep brown oval eyes with full cheeks. Long, slender nose with pouted lips. She was petite, but not too thick for her size. A long, slender neck with narrow shoulders that her uniform looked well on. Smooth, bronze skin showed from places that was not covered with cloth. Firm, sleek legs sprouted from beneath her skirt.

She noticed him staring before he had a chance to look away and smiled.

"Can I help you with something?"
"I'm sorry for staring, but I can't help but tell you that you're a very beautiful woman. I hope it doesn't sound like a line, but I couldn't help but stare, your beauty is breathtaking."
She laughed. "Thank you. It's very seldom a man comes out honestly and tells how they feel after they have gawked at a woman. And it DOES sound like a line."

He laughed as she sipped her drink.

"Honestly," he reassured her. "I only speak the truth. Can I interest you in another drink or perhaps my name?" I feel that is the least I can do for being so rude. The name is Pierre, Pierre Mason."
"Nice to meet you, Mr. Mason," she said, shaking his hand. "I'll take you up on the offer."
"Another one of what she is having," he announced to the bartender.
"A coke please."
"Excuse me," he continued. "I didn't catch your name?"
"I didn't give it to you."

He looked surprised. She continued. "I don't feel comfortable meeting men in airports. They feel as if flight attendants come as an added bonus with their getaway trips."
"I'm on business."
"On business, too," she added. "If you really desire to know my name, it's got to be in a better place than this, I'm sorry."

She got up and left, without even drinking the coke he bought. He look at the bartender, he shrugged his shoulders and continued to clean a glass, then he turned and watched her walk away.

She was a strong, black woman. Feisty, young, and very independent by the way she carried herself. And even though he was turned down, he felt strangely attracted to her. He hadn't felt this way since when he first met his wife. Her feistiness attracted him as well as her independence. He loved a challenge and she was promising.

They announced his flight number over the airport intercom system. It was boarding. He finished his drink, tipped the bar, then headed for his departure gate.

As he boarded the plane, he was greeted by the woman he met in the bar. She was the flight attendant on his flight! He walked over to her and as she welcomed him on the airline, leaned over and whispered in her ear, "I liked the other place better."

She smiled at him as she directed him toward his seat. *This is gonna be a long flight*, Pierre thought as he watched her help other people get settled.

ROB

There comes a point in every love affair when, so it seem, the woman gets pissed off at her lover being happy. Sure she know its her making him happy. Sure she knows that its her pleasure, even her job. But finally she comes to the conclusion that in some way, he is getting away with murder. Especially with the man married and the woman not. For then relationship is an answer to his problem, but does not solve hers.

Shelley had come to that stage. For nearly two weeks Rob managed to sidetrack her to avoid the conversation, but it was inevitable. Usually she was pissed off that he stayed married and didn't make any promises for a permanent commitment.

They were in her apartment after the movies. It was late. From her bedroom they could look and see the city lights.

"Let's go to bed," Rob said. He was dying to make love to her. He was always dying to make love to her.
"Damn," Shelley said. "You always want to fuck!"
"No," Rob said. "I want to make love to you."
He had become that sentimental. She looked at him coldly, but her liquid brown eyes was flashing with anger.
"You and your fucking innocence," she said. "Fuck you!"

But she laughed.

And what led to all of this was that Rob never lied to her. And she wanted him to lie. She wanted him to give her all the bullshit married men give to women they fuck. Like "my wife and I are getting a divorce." Like "my wife and I haven't fucked in years." Like "my wife and I have an understanding." Like "my wife and I are unhappy." Since none of this was true for Rob, he wouldn't say it. He loved his wife, they shared the same bedroom, had sex, they were happy. He had the best of two worlds and he wasn't going to give it up. So much the worse for him.

Once Shelley laughed she was OK for a while. So now she went and drew a tub full of hot water. They always took a bath together before they went to bed. She would wash him and he would wash her and they'd fool around a little and then jump out and dry each other, with big towels. Then they'd wind themselves around each other, naked under the covers.

But tonight was different. After they made love she snuggled close to him.

"That's why I love you," Shelley said. "You really do understand me."

"I do, baby. Let's go to sleep," Rob said.

"You know I love you really and truly," Shelley said.

"Yeah," Rob said.

"And you don't think I'm a bitch for complaining, do you?" Shelley asked.

"Nope," Rob said. "Let's go to sleep." He reached out to hold her.

She moved a little.

84

"Why don't you leave your wife and marry me? Tell me the truth."

"Because I have it both ways," Rob said.

"You bastard." She poked him in the balls with her finger. It hurt.

"Damn," Rob said. "Just because I'm madly in love with you, just because I like to talk to you better than anybody, what makes you think I'd leave my wife for you."

She didn't know whether Rob serious or not. She decided he was kidding. It was a dangerous assumption to make.

"Very seriously," Shelley said. "Honestly, I just want to know. Why do you still stay married to your wife? Give me one good reason."

Rob rolled into a protective ball before he answered. "Because she's not a bitch,"

15

PIERRE

All during the flight to Miami, Michelle was constantly swamped with advances from Pierre. He was kind, humorous, and she like how he played to win her confidence over. Finally she consented to showing him around Miami after he completed his business. But she had no intentions of falling in love. Men at this particular time had no part in her life except friendship. She had gave up in the game a long time ago and was content with her marriage with work. She enjoyed her job as a stewardess at Delta Airlines and was considered one of the best. She strived to be the best in everything for as long as she could remember.

When she was young, being the oldest in her family of four, her mother and father took pride in her and instilled hard working ethics in her. In high school, she was very work orientated, earning good grades and graduating in the top one percent of her class. Socially she had many friends and was very popular, but guys shied away from her because of her beauty, assuming she had boyfriends and was stuck up. College was different. She dated many men, but they took advantage of her and used her. After college, she gave up trying to find the right man and fell mostly for her work. Since she loved to travel, she loved her job

86

and seldom took time off for herself except an occasional visit to see her parents and her sister. After constant talks with her mom, she concluded she was enjoying life, but was missing something that's important in everyone's life; someone to love. She almost gave up searching till Pierre walked into her life. She was attracted to him, but wanted to see if there was more to him except looks.

As everyone boarded off the plane and was waiting around the conveyor for their luggage, Pierre walked up to her.

"Was I a pain in the ass on the flight?" He inquired politely.

She smiled. "You wasn't as bad as the guy in coach. Actually, I enjoyed having you on the flight."

He laughed. "You say that to everyone on the flight."

"No, I really mean it," she assured him. "I enjoyed your company and if you have time in your busy schedule I'll be glad to take you up on that invitation. I'll be here for week. Here's my address."

She pulled a piece of paper from a small memo pad and wrote her address and number on it and handed it to him.

"So it's a date," Pierre suggested.

"No, its a tour, Michelle instructed. "Let's not get confused with what you asked me."

"Date, tour, whatever's fine with me, Miss Carter," added Pierre, glancing at the note. "Can I call you tomorrow?"

"Certainly. And you can even call me Michelle, too."

"Have a nice evening, Michelle," said Pierre, smiling as he walked away.

You too, she thought as she watched him walked away. Something strangely attracted her to him. He was different, and now curious, she wanted to know more. Turning as her crew came off the plane, she hurried to gather her luggage, and joined them.

16

ROB

The late hours Rob kept with Shelley were not lost on his wife. Marie herself was now spending as much time as she could away from home. She was always out with friends, shopping, going to exercise classes, visiting her parents, or going to the movies. She left him dinners to warm up when he chose to come home, and little notes informing him of her whereabouts.

Even though her absence and silence told him she knew something was up, he thought it was helping him facilitate his relations with Shelley. While his marriage was slowly crumbling.

The few times he spent with her, they got into arguments. They argued over money spent, the kid, about the change in his job, and him coming home at odd hours. Both of them knew what they were really fighting about, but neither of them wished to address it directly.

The only time they didn't argue was when they slept. This was because distance was greater between them at night. Marie curled up on her side of the bed while Rob lay awake on his side.

Rob was deeply sad about what was happening. He had always loved Marie for her level head, her humor, and her strength as a wife and mother. She married him when they were both in college and while he strived to be the best, she interrupted her education to help him.

Everyday he used to look forward to the smile she greeted him when he came home. Now the smile was gone, because she never acknowledged his presence. He couldn't tell her how much this hurt cause he knew he deserved it.

His son was not even aware of the situation. She made sure of that as he spent afternoons, and evenings at the home of her mother. The family was falling apart and no one wanted to be in the house anymore. And even though he knew the solution to the problem, he could not tear himself away from Shelley.

One evening he came home late after a mid shift and Marie alone, waiting for him. She sat on the love seat in the living room, looking at him with such authority that he sat down to hear her out.

"I know you've been sleeping with Shelley," she said.
He began to deny it, but she quieted him with one look and a raise of her hand.
"Don't make yourself look stupid by denying it Rob," she said. "She called me tonight...Not that she needed to."
She forced herself to go on. He looked at her guiltily. The only thing harder to behold than the reproach in her eyes was

the pain. She wasn't looking at him, but at the monster that had come between them, that was killing her family.

"I've given this matter a lot of thought the past couple of weeks," she said. "For six years you were the best husband I thought a woman could be lucky to have, Rob. I loved you. And I've decided, I still love you. So I'm giving you one chance, and one chance only to make it right between us, for ourselves, and for the sake of our son. There are three lives at stake here. If you wish to ruin yours, fine, but I intend to save the other two."

Rob tried to swallow, but couldn't force the lump down that was stuck in his throat.
"What do you want me to do to get things back the way it was?" He asked.
"I want you to move out tomorrow to get your head on straight, don't worry, we both need this time away from each other to think. And I want you to end it with her, right away. Then I want my Rob back the way he used to be, with Christian and me. It's that simple.

Rob thought for a long moment. Marie's courage was so touching and a human thing that it almost brought tears to his eyes. He weighed everything at stake, seeing things for the first time. He took a deep breath and stood up.

"All right, baby."

From her seat his wife gave him a look that pierced his heart cold. Then she got up, turned out the light, and went to bed.

Rob stood alone in the silent living room. The next move was his.

17

MARCUS

The next morning Marcus was awakened by the persistent buzzing of the doorbell. Someone was at the door. He glanced groggily at the intercom that was flashing on the wall, then raised up out of the bed and pressed the button.

"Yeah."
"Hey baby, I brought some of my things over, buzz me up."
Dominique.
"Baby, it's 8:30 in the morning."
"I know it is early," she explained. "I wanted to start moving in now so we can have the evening to settled in."
"Okay, wait. I'll help you."

He pressed the button to let her up, then slipped on a T-shirt and shoes. She met him at the foot of the stairs and hugged him.

"Thanks baby, I am so happy," she declared, kissing him on the cheek.
I'm glad someone is, thought Marcus as he embraced her, then went outside to carry her things inside.

****

Couple hours later, they were finished. Marcus was busy taking a shower while Dominique was unpacking boxes, getting settled. The phone rang just as Marcus was getting out of the shower.

"I got it!" he shouted as he wrapped a towel around his wet body, running to the phone in the bedroom. I need to get my phone number changed, he thought as he picked up the phone.
"Hello?"
"Yo, baby boy this is Rob."
"What's up?"
"I need a favor."
"Anything."
"I need to stay with you for a while."
"What happened?"

So Rob told Marcus, starting from how he started sexing Shelley and she was demanding more time, not leaving anything out till when she called his wife and she kicked him out. When he finished, Marcus was laughing.

"Got hooked on the pussy, huh?"
"It was YOUR advice I took and look where it has gotten me!" Rob snapped. "Can I stay or what?"
"Look, I'd let you stay, but Dominique has just moved in."
"What?" Rob teased. "Not Mr. Mack Daddy himself trying to chill."
"Temporarily," Marcus countered. "I don't think it's gonna work. I need space, you know me."

92

"I know you're fucking up," Rob continued. "So where am I gonna stay?"

"Pierre is out of town for a while, use his crib. He gave you the keys, right?"

"Right."

"So you have a place. But you need to clean that shit up before he gets back. You have a week."

"I know. You gonna at least help me move are you?"

"Can't," Marcus said flatly. "You know Marie is gonna think I put you up to that shit. I'm out on this one."

"So you're gonna leave me hanging?"

"Like Jordan in a slam dunk contest. Sorry, I'm busy, so holla at me later okay, peace."

Marcus hung up, then thought how wrong that was. Rob needed him. He'll get over it, he thought as he walked back to the bathroom to dry off.

"Who was that?" Dominique inquired politely as she walked in the bathroom.

Marcus explained. "That was Rob. He's in a jam and asked to stay over here for a while. I turned him down."

"You should have helped him, he's your friend."

"Okay, he can stay, you can leave," Marcus said flatly.

"I'm not leaving!" Dominique snapped.

"Then he's not staying. We have to get used to staying together. Three's a crowd."

"You mean you have to get used to me being around."

Marcus shot her a look, then turned and started shaving. Dominique watched him shave. She liked being around him, but she had the feeling that he thinks she's trying to control him. To take control of his life. She didn't want to take control, but just be a part of his life. She'll make him understand. But for now, she just wanted to make him happy.

Coming up behind him, she grabbed his butt, then hugged him and laid her head on his shoulder.

"Have I told you that I love you today?" She suggested.

"The day just started-"

"And I want us to start off on the right foot," she interjected. "What are you doing today?"

"I have a photo shoot at one, why?"

She gazed at him through the mirror.

"I was thinking we'd celebrate this day with some good loving," she said shyly, kissing him on his back.

"Well, that job is pretty much my day, so I guess I'll take you up on that offer."

He turned facing her and touched her on the nose, leaving a dab of shaving cream on it. She smiled, content with what he said and grabbed his crotch. Stroking him slowly, she kissed him on the chest and looked up at him.

"This is how I want us to get started," she purred. "I'll meet you in the bedroom."

She walked off, leaving articles of clothing here and there as she went upstairs. Marcus shook his head as he quickly finished shaving, then went up after her.

18

PIERRE

Pierre showed up at Copeland Enterprises an hour early. His creative team was there already, waiting on him in the lobby. He wanted his first impression, also his first presentation, to be flawless, so he worked late into the night looking over everything. As he pushed through the double glass doors, his personal assistant, Byron, met with a nervous look.

"When will they let us know?" Bryon demanded for the tenth time that week.

"We have the account, relax." Pierre responded. "Whether the boards approves of our presentation is something you can't project. But when they do, news will travel fast."

"There's something profoundly sarcastic about all of this," Bryon said. "Nobody gets a seven million dollar account without a little suffering, that's the price of the game. It's sadistic, but I bet every industry has these little cruel habits."

"Not at Burke and Burke."

"Do you think we should pray?"

"We don't pray for business success, or at least I don't think we do. Does this elevator run or what?" Pierre asked impatiently as he pressed the button continuously.

They got in the elevator and discussed their strategy as they went up. When it opened, three of the reps from Copeland joined them in the lobby on the 7th floor, two of them dressed softly in full throttle Armani, the third more chastely business-like than ever in a perfectly plain navy suit that could have been cut by Hugo Boss with his own hands.

The board of directors, not bothering to pretend to make conversations, found the seventh floor meeting room with ease. Pierre and his team was greeted by a dignified, middle- aged woman who introduced herself as Karyn, Executive Assistant to the President of Copeland Enterprises, Dexter Copeland.

"Make yourselves comfortable," Karyn said with a pleasant smile. "The bosses are running late. Can I get you coffee or tea? No? There are pitchers of water at your table, let me know if you run out."

Pierre surveyed the room. At one end was a group of chairs for the audience, at the other end a simple table with five chairs behind it and an easel at each side. To the far wall, a large video monitor and podium where he would probably run his presenta-tion.

Pierre sat down in the center chair, flanked by Byron and his two people, carrying large portfolios filled with their carefully mockup ads, sat at each end.

After a short wait, a group of people entered from the con-necting rooms. Karyn rose to make presentations. First came the Copeland brothers, who owned Copeland Enterprises, Deon, Dwayne, and Dexter, who was the senior brother and clearly the most important of the three. Then came the marketing director with her male assistant. As the three brothers took their seats in the second row, three somberly dressed, dumpy older women sat down in the last row.

The Copeland brothers, Pierre thought, either hired their secretaries for their efficiency, or their wives hired them for safety. As far as he could judge, the brothers were all in their mid to late thirties, and each of them had a strong family resemblance to each other. And impassive. He had never seen such a lack of expression, neither bored nor anticipatory, but empty of everything except the steady almost unblinking attention of their eyes.

Their faces remained blank as Bryon explained how Burke and Burke with its clever researchers and state-of-the-art media buying department was bringing Copeland Enterprises to a new level.

Then Pierre spoke, presenting other aspects of why Burke and Burke will take them to another level of advertising, including his Cambridge Awards for artwork.

"Now Bryon, Chris, and Kim, my creative team will show the ads and presentation they've prepared that will take Copeland Enterprises to new heights."

In the next fifteen minutes, his team went to work, showing them sketches, ads, and passing portfolios. The last five minutes Pierre took the floor and showed the video presentation that his clients approved of so much they desired his presence there. A standing ovation of applauds swept over the presentation room as Pierre finished. Dexter Copeland rose and shook his hand, thanking him.

"I like your work," Dexter Copeland said, with grave approval, sweeping his eyes over the creative team. As soon as he spoke, his personal power was evident.

"There is no need to wait and tell you that this account is only one in more to come. We want you to represent every new product that comes on line. This is only the first. We're going to enjoy our relationship with Burke and Burke."

"Thank you," Pierre said, since everyone else seemed to have lost their voices. "We won't let you down."

"Of course we'll need a representative down here to keep up updated on all current projects and I'll look forward to your visits also. I'll call your boss tomorrow and we'll set another date to get online with you."

Around them the Copeland Enterprise people were shaking hands with the creative team, laughing and talking in an explosion of tension they had all been under, but around Dexter Copeland and Pierre there was a circle of respect everyone instinctively accorded to what had transpired in the room that day.

WANTING EYES

****

Some time later that afternoon Pierre arrived at the Regency, a hotel where he was staying. It was located approximately two blocks away from Miami Beach and in the center of the main shopping district. Hurrying inside, he couldn't wait to relay the good news. His office at home was ecstatic; His boss elated; now he wanted to share the good news with his friends.

He called Rob at home, only to find out he was put out. Listening to Marie talking and crying on the phone, he could only contain his own pain, knowing how she felt. Then defending Rob, he said a few words of comfort and hung up. Sighing, he called his place cause he knew that was the only place he could go. Marcus wouldn't dream of helping him.
The phone rang four times before his answering machine picked it up. Listening to the message, it ended, and with a beep he started talking. Rob doesn't want to answer the phone.

"Rob! Pick up man! We need to talk. Rob-"
"Yeah, what's up man?" Rob said, interrupting the recording message with a beep. "Look, I know what your gonna say-"
"No you don't. Stop trippin. It's happened and now it is up to you. You can stay as long as you like, just make things right, okay. You have a good woman. Any other female and your ass would have been to the curb. Handle your business."
"All right. Thanks for letting me stay."
"Anything for a brother. Look the presentation went well, I had those guys drooling, and I met a woman."
"What!"

So Pierre started telling him how he met Michelle at the airport, and didn't stop till he told him she gave up the digits.

"Rob, I swear she made me feel like I was a teenager again. It was something special. Unspoken, but we both knew it was meant."

"So?"

"So what?"

"Did you hit it?"

"Look man, we haven't even went out yet. I'm going to ask her out tonight. Since I'm chillin for a week, I'm going to spend some time with her."

"What about Sandra?"

"Our relationship is open, I'm going to tell her about Michelle, why?"

"She called me when I was at home asking if you have called."

"So?"

"So she's been worrying Marcus too. I think you need to call her."

"I told her I'd call her as soon as I was settled, I guess I forgot in all the excitement here. I'll call as soon as we hang up."

"Well, I'm out. I gotta get ready for work and then I have to handle my business."

"Do that. And be careful."

"All right, peace."

"Peace."

Pierre hung up and thought for a moment before calling. Tell Sandra over the phone about a woman would be too impersonal, as if the argument they had awhile ago, complicated their relationship. She's probably already upset from not calling soon enough. After considering everything, weighing it as if it was a hard decision, he decided to wait until he came home to tell her.

He dialed Sandra's number then waited. She answered the
phone after two rings.

"Hello?"

"Hey San, what's up?"

"What's up with you? Sandra snapped. "How come it took
you so long to call? I was worried something happened."

Pierre explained. "Well, the meeting took longer than I
thought, then I had to call Rob to make sure everything was
okay. I just got off the phone with him and called you."

"Did he tell you I called him?"

"Yeah."

"So why didn't you call me first? Oh, I'm sorry, your job,
your friends, then me is that it?"

"That's not true."

"Probably not. But what is true to me is your inability to
keep your word."

"I called as soon as I got settled. I don't know what your
problem is, but I really don't feel like arguing about something
trivial."

"So I'm trivial, is that what you're saying?"

"No! I'm saying what we're discussing is trivial."

They argued back and forth, with it ending with Sandra
hanging up in his face. He paused before he hung up, just listening to the dial tone. Trying to please Sandra and understand
where she was coming from was just too much for him

.

Hanging the phone up, he sat there, thinking where they were
going with what was left with their relationship. Sighing, he decided to enjoy the week in Miami and deal with her later. But
for now, he wanted to make every minute count.

Picking up the phone, he called Michelle and made plans to
see her. With anticipation and growing excitement of being with

her, he showered, and changed in something casual, then mixed a drink at the bar.

Sitting down to relax, he contemplated about the evening he was going to have with Michelle. She attracted him true enough, but there was something oddly familiar about her, and he was determined to know all about her.

19

MARCUS

Despite the hour, Marcus returned home late. He knew Dominique would be pissed, cause she wanted to celebrate moving in with him. Think of a good excuse, he thought was he unloaded his equipment, and put the roll of film that needed processing in the dark room. If this is what marriage life is all about, I don't need it, he thought as he walked upstairs.

"Baby, daddy's home," he proclaimed as he came upstairs. There was no answer.

"Baby, I can explain," he suggested as he made his way to the bedroom.

No one there. No messages on the answer machine, no notes. She probably stepped out for a minute, he thought as he undressed and ran water to take a shower. As he took off his jewelry he glanced at his full length mirror. There to his surprise was a note, written in her lipstick. Curious, he walked over and read it.

Dear Marcus,
I found an earring while cleaning under the couch in the liv-
ing room.
I always knew you were fooling around but I could never
bring myself to confront you.
Maybe I didn't want to hear the truth. No need to explain or
make up excuses.
It would only add pain to my broken heart.
I loved you more than I ever loved anyone in my life.
But I cannot see you again.
I'll come by later to pick up the rest of my things and leave
the keys.
I really thought we had true love, that I had a real man.
But I know now that this man is a boy that loves to play.
In time you'll realize you lost a good thing, but until then you
will never be satisfied.
And you'll never know how hurt I am.
Dominique

Upset, he sat down on the bed and rubbed his forehead with his hand. The earring that Monique lost and he had failed to find came back to haunt him miserably. Sighing, he laid back on the bed and pressed the speed dial number to Dominique.

The phone rang until her answer machine pick up with a beep.

"Baby, please don't go away mad, I can explain. You know I don't like talking into answering machine, but if you're home pick up, we need to talk."

He listened.

"Okay, call me as soon as you get home, I'll be waiting."

He hung up. *When shit hits the fan, it spreads all over the place*, he thought as he finished undressing, then went to take a shower.

20

ROB

When Rob got his first look as his desk as he walked into his office Friday evening, he was reminded of the headache he left of his desk. A lot of things passed through his mind within a week's time that put his new job on the back burner......until to-day.

He picked up the admission log and glanced over it as he sat down. Making a mental note to make rounds as soon as he cleared his desk, he went to work, but his mind was preoccupied with the situation he faced at home. Tears clouded his eyes as he thought how he hurt Marie. He admired her courage and the way she controlled her destiny. That was one of the things he loved about her. But now the decision rested on his shoulders, and in his state of confusion, he was hesitant to end the relation-ship.

Sexually, Shelley satisfied his every need, and that was basi-cally the cornerstone of the rapidly built relationship, but he wasn't ready to end it yet, despite Marie's knowing. But the line was drawn, the ball in his court, and Marie was waiting to see what kind of return he had.

He knew it was going to come to this, he had made a lot of mistakes that made it painstakingly obvious to everyone. Now the time had come for a serious talk that he had been avoiding with Shelley for weeks.

He picked up the phone and dialed her number. After several rings she picked up.

"Hello," she whispered in a sleepy voice.

"You sleep?"

"Hey baby. Yeah I was, but I need to get up, how are you?"

"We need to talk."

"If this is about my call I figured that if you couldn't leave her, I should let her know about us."

"I was getting around to it."

"Yeah, that's what they all say when they're getting what they want, I just made sure there would be no excuses for you to see the light."

"But there is a right way and a-"

"There is no right way," interjected Shelley. "You're married with a child. Obliviously she's not qualified to take care of you like I can, so let's cut through the bull. I don't fuck around, I want a man, and you're qualified. I helped you now only thing you have to do is move out."

"I was kicked out on my ass last week!" snapped Rob.

"And there is a warm bed waiting on you with me in it," purred Shelley. "Want me to tell you what I'm wearing?"

"No, I need to come over and talk."

"Okay, then come over. I'll be waiting."

Rob hung up. He was getting nowhere on the phone and talking to her only made him angry. Snatching his things, he left hurriedly, leaving his briefcase in the office, knowing he would settle things with no problems and be back to work before anyone misses him.

21

PIERRE

Friday evening promptly at eight o'clock, Pierre arrived at Michelle's hotel in a rented gray BMW. Michelle was waiting in the lobby when he came in to greet her.

She was wearing a beautiful dark blue summer dress, pretty, but not too enticing so she wouldn't be taken cheap. She hadn't been on a date for more than fourteen months, and she nearly forgotten how to dress for the occasion; she had spent nearly two hours choosing her outfit, as indecisive as a schoolgirl.

She accepted Pierre's invitation because he was the most interesting man she'd met in a couple of years - and also she was trying her best to overcome her tendency to put men down. She had been hurt by her mother's assessment of her; she had told her that she was using her self-reliance as an excuse to hide and she had recognized the truth in what she'd said.

She had friends but avoided finding lovers, because she was afraid of the pain that only lovers inflict with betrayal and rejection. But at the same time she was protecting herself from pain, she was denying herself the pleasure of good relations with good men who would not betray her. Growing up going through bad relationships, she had learned that displays of affections were usually followed by those same unexpected endings.

She was never afraid to take chances in her work and business matters; now it was time to bring the same emotion in her personal life.

As she walked toward Pierre, swinging her hips a little, she felt tense about taking an emotional risk that dating entailed, but she also felt happier than she had in a long time.

They went outside to where his car was parked. Pierre hurried to the passenger side and opened the door. Bending low and putting his arm behind his back, he said, "Enter my African queen."

"Oh, there must be some mistake, I'm not your African queen."

"Well, you look like an African queen, if you are not mine."

"I'm just a lowly airline stewardess."

"And a beautiful one at that."

Michelle groaned.

"I take it you've heard it all before. Too corny?" He asked.

"I need some butter after that one."

"But you liked it."

"As much as a pap smear," she said, getting into the BMW in a swirl of blue.

As they drove off, Pierre asked, "You're not upset are you?"

"About what?"

"By me trying to impress you."

"No, just don't try to, be yourself, that's what I like."

"Okay, I'll impress you next week."

"You seem pretty sure we'll still be kickin it next week."

"Why wouldn't we be?" He asked.

"Maybe we'll get into a fight, tonight, first thing at the restaurant."

"Over what?"

"Well," she said. "Maybe we're the kind of people that argue over little things."

"Such as?"

"Well, the food, the type of restaurant. Maybe you'll hate the food and I'll like it."

"No, I have the feeling that whatever you choose to go, I'll like it, but we'll have to wait and see."

She told him where to go, giving him directions as he drove.

They arrived at the Blue Dragon restaurant, just off the main strip. It was an intimate place, seating no more that thirty and somehow appearing to seat only half that number; It was cozy, comfortable, the kind of place you would lose track of time and spend hours over dinner if the waiters didn't bother you. The lighting was soft and warm. The music was soulful jazz by Miles Davis - played loud enough to be heard and appreciated, but not so loud that it interrupted conversation.

The host, after escorting them to a table, had the waiters take their orders. One waiter returned with a bottle of Don Perignon as the host waited for the wine, and uncorked it himself. After the glasses had been filled and a toast made, he left them, winking at Michelle to show his approval. Pierre noticed him winking as he left.

"You know him?"

"He is a good friend of mine."

"And he doesn't want to be with you?"

"He's gay."

"Oh," Pierre said, looking over to where he was standing.

He noticed Pierre staring, laughed to himself, then winked at him.

"I see why you act the way you do," said Pierre, shaking his head.

"Why did you say that? He doesn't ask me for nothing, and he definitely won't compromise a friendship for a piece, like other friends I used to have."

They fell smoothly into talking about men and then their jobs. She was so easy to talk to that Pierre felt he known her for years. There was absolutely none of the awkwardness that comes with first dates.

The food was nearly as good as the conversation. The appetizer was light; it consists of spicy beef wrapped in cabbage. Their oriental greens salad were huge and crisp, smothered in vinaigrette dressing. Pierre selected the sweet sour stir fried chicken. The ice coffee was excellent.

When they finished dinner and Pierre looked at his watch, he was amazed to see that it was ten minutes past eleven.

"You busy tomorrow?" Michelle asked.
"Not really."
"Want to go dancing? I know some good places. "
"I'd like that."

Fifteen minutes later, they arrived at one of Michelle's favorite places, the Warehouse, where sounds of Hip Hop and R&B

was floating out into the parking lot. Making their way to the front of the line, they were escorted in by two large bouncers.

Pierre looked Michelle and pointed at them.

"You know them?"
"Yep."
"I'd hate to see someone get on your bad side."

Michelle laughed.

They went inside and was greeted by Steve, manager of the club. After being seated in the VIP section and wine brought to their table, Pierre turned to face her.

"I'm really enjoying myself, thanks for showing me around."
She nodded.

"I'm enjoying this as much as you are, believe me."
"I'll believe you when we dance, come on."

He rose and took her by the hand and together they walked to the dance floor. As they started dancing, the music slowed down as the DJ changed the music to a slow song. With the sounds of Jodeci "Stay" in their ears, they glanced unexpectantly at each other as, knowingly, they decided to slow dance.

The music swirled around them like a throbbing haze of sound as he grasped her by the wrist. Raising her hand palm up, he pressed his lips to the soft place at the base of her palm where the blood beats closest to the skin's surface. For a second, she felt the blood coursing up, up through her veins. Then he lifted his head and looked into her eyes. Her knees felt a little weak as she stared back at him. Relaxing in the comfort of his strong arms, she let him lead as she closed her eyes and enjoyed the moment. It had been a long time since she danced with a man this close that she felt she could stay in his arms forever.

The rest of the night was like a blur, a swirling, hazy dream as they danced and talked intimately all night.

They left the club and walked about three blocks to a waffle house that stayed open 24 hours. There they ordered breakfast and coffee. Staring at Michelle as the waiter picked up their menus and left, Pierre reached across the table and took her hand into his.

"So did you enjoy yourself?" He inquired politely.
"I enjoyed myself, very much thank you. Your very fun to be with."
"And you are a fabulous, beautiful host that I enjoyed keeping company. So do you think this will continue?"
Michelle put her fingers on Pierre's lips to silence him.
"Let's not discuss that now. Let's just enjoy the moment."

They ate breakfast in silence, as if knowing the attraction between them was strong without words. After they ate, they left walking slowly hand in hand beneath the starry sky.

The sky was clear and dark, like a dark velvet cloth, besetted with sparkling jewels. He drove her to her hotel and walked her to the door.

"I enjoyed myself immensely. This was a wonderful night. Can I come up with you to talk?"

He smiled mischievously.

"I enjoyed myself too, but I can't. I'm sorry, I just can't go out like that on the first date."

"That's okay, that's cool, I'll call you tomorrow."

"Okay, that's fine."

They moved slowly, almost hesitantly towards each other, and they kissed passionately, almost urgently, but with the wanton desire to kiss. She pulled away.

"Okay, that's enough before you start something."

"I'm sorry."

"There is nothing to be sorry about, believe me."

He smiled, turned and walked away. She watched him leave, then turned around.

"Michelle."

She turned and looked into the most pleading eyes.

"Can I? Just talk?" He stood smiling with his arms outstretched.

"Good night Pierre."

She turned and walked away. He stood watching, shook his head, and walked to the car.

22

ROB

Within an hour, Rob arrived at Shelley's apartment complex. Hurrying inside, he walked briskly to the elevator and impatiently pushed the elevator button while glancing at his watch. He was taking a big risk leaving the job without anyone knowing his whereabouts and he knew it.

I cannot be longwinded, he thought to his self. *I have to be straightforward and direct.* Thinking to himself over and over, he paced back and forth as the elevator descended, and with a ring, opened its doors invitingly.

Pacing back and forth inside the elevator, Rob rehearsed what he was going to say to Shelley, as if he was preparing for a part in a school play. But mostly he had to psyche himself up to go through with telling her without succumbing to her wiles.

Shelley was a seductively beautiful, intelligent woman that knew how to use her womanly charms to get what she wants.

Before Shelley had called his wife, Rob had tried to have a serious discussion with her about their relationship, but it had ended in an intense lovemaking episode that further confused his already clouded mind to what he wanted to say but couldn't. He

115

went home that night more confused than he was when he arrived. This time he was not going to let it happen.

His thoughts was broken by the abrupt, but soft landing of the elevator, followed by a ring and the doors opening.

He stood there, pausing as if to change his mind. But thinking how his wife looked at him that fateful night, caused him to go on. He found himself knocking on her apartment door.

No answer.

He knocked again then checked the door knob. It was unlocked. Now where did she go? He thought as he opened the door and let himself into a dark apartment. There were no lights on in neither the living room, nor the kitchen. Only the faint ticking of the clock on the kitchen wall.

"Shelley, are you here?" He asked, in almost a whisper. Nothing.

He walked in the hallway and seen a dim light flicker from the cracked doorway of her bedroom. He walked slowly down the hallway and opened the door partly. There, lying on the bed, surfing through the channels on the TV, was Shelley.

She looked beautiful with her hair slightly messed and in one of his large shirts he had left over there.

"Hey baby, what took you so long?" Asked Shelley as she turned the TV off, then turned the stereo on, loud enough to be heard and appreciated, but not loud enough to interrupt their conversation. "I thought you changed your mind. You know if something happens while you are not at the hospital, you'll be held liable. But I like it. It's making me horny. Unauthorized

116

absence to be with his lover." She caressed her body slowly, almost teasingly, tempting him.

"You know that is not why I came," Rob said as he rubbed his eyes slowly, then refocused on her.

"Oh yeah, you want to talk," Shelley said as she sat up and patted on the bed. "Come on baby, make yourself comfortable."

He hesitated.

"I'm not going to bite if that is what you're thinking,"

She smiled mischievously.

"That's not what I'm worried about."

He sat down beside her on the bed and gazed into her eyes. Silhouetted by the dim light, she looked radiant, warm, compelling. He had the urge to wrap his arm around her. To hold her. To kiss her. He broke his gaze and looked away.

"Shelley, I have feelings for you, but I don't love you. Love makes one feel connected to everything, and safe in the world. I don't what to live without it. I'm saying this to say that I don't want to live without Marie in my life. You and I shared something special, but it was more lust than love. After the sex, we have nothing, cause our relationship was built on sex. I could never leave Marie for you."

He looked at her for an expression, a sign that he had made her come to an understanding that she should let go, but there was only silent pleading in her eyes.

Shelley spoke. "Baby, when we make love, it seems our bodies would not be adequate to express our desire to be with each other...., in each other.

She kissed him slowly, her tongue wandered, searching within his mouth. She broke away and hugged him.

"But our lovemaking is adequate and we touch each other's insides,".

...

She took his hands and slowly with her hands over his, traced her breasts and stomach. Then she sucked on one of his fingers, as her other hand guided his other hand down to her love.

"In our innermost self".....

She guided his fingers inside her as she moaned. They kissed passionately, hungrily. The music suffocated them like a cloud of heat as he kissed her on the neck, teased her with his tongue on her breasts, then trailed his tongue down slowly toward her navel.

Shelley gasped and whimpered as his tongue traced along the outside of her naval. Then sucking on her navel deeply, he stopped and sat up in the bed.

Shelley raised up, breathing hard.

"What's wrong?" Why did you stop?"
"I just realized I have a wonderful, strong woman that loves me very much despite what I've done. I love her very much, and it wasn't until this very moment that I realized it.
Shelley sighed with frustration and lay back in bed.

"Well, if you love her so much, what are you doing here with me?"

He turned and looked into her eyes. "Exactly."

He rose up and left her apartment, not once glancing back.

WANTING EYES

****

At last he returned to work, feeling relieved, but with mixed emotions. There were things that he and Marie done once upon a time in their marriage that he and Shelley did. But with child, his job, and falling into an everyday routine, made the romance fizzle out in their once burning relationship. He realized that the romance never died in their relationship, they only exhausted the possibilities. Determined to reignite the flames of romance in their relationship, he picked up the phone and called home.

Marie answered the phone after two rings.
"Hello?"
"Hey baby, we need to talk."
"I can't right now. I have to pick up Christian from school. Can you call me back?"
"Please just give me five minutes, and just listen okay?"
"Okay, your on the clock."

He took a deep breath. "Baby, I was calling because I want my void to be filled. To fill my empty heart with your sweet voice. I am a soulless man, wandering aimlessly in confusion over what has happened between us. I guess if you didn't love me so much it wouldn't have hurt. Like a baby in a mother's arms I need you, and my life would be worth living. I'm calling because I want you to know how I feel, about everything that has happened, but mostly about you and I, and our future. Truly within my heart I am a changed man, and with that change became the understanding of self and others. I guess you held me within the likeness of you. For that it hurt you that I betrayed you. I say all this to say that I want to be a part of your life again. You are my angel of love, my gift of life. Like water in a river flowing towards the sea, I am drawn to you. Like a moth swarming around a flame, I want to feel the warmth of your love again. Never in my life have I felt such a perfect love. Our love is special cause it grew from a spark long ago to a the burning flame it is today."

He continued. "But my fear is one question; what is today? Because one month in the chapter of our lives has changed into a question that will forever change my soul. I can say my soul because I know what is within my heart. I called to ask you what was within your heart that is still alive with my love. Of only a spark, I will care for it, tend it, and feed it love so once again we can travel over the winds of love that our doves once flew. But I need to hear it from you. I'll let you go, bye baby."

He hung up with tears in his eyes, unknowing that he was not the only one crying.

23

MARCUS

The beauty salon was crowded with more women than Marcus imagined. He stood outside the door, wide-eyed in amazement and excitement as women came and went, looking beautiful than ever. Women under hair dryers, women tilted back in chairs with their hair getting shampooed, women getting manicures, pedicures, and facials.

This is a bad idea, thought Marcus as he paced impatiently on the sidewalk in front of his car. I have a perfect explanation for what happened, but she hasn't been answering her phone. Maybe if I apologize in front of all these women, I'll gain big sympathy points, thought Marcus as he walked to the door, opened it to let a women pass, then went it.

Marcus walked up to the receptionist desk and politely inquired about Dominique. A brightly dressed, voluptuously plump sista with long braid extensions in her hair turned in her chair facing him, and without interrupting her phone conversation, pointed a well manicured finger in the direction where Dominique was. Then, turning her back to Marcus, continued talking as if he wasn't there.

Dominique was sitting in a chair with her head tilted back in a sink, while her beautician was shampooing her hair. Marcus smiled at the sight as he walked over to where she was sitting.

"Baby, we need to talk."

Dominique raised her head slightly to see who was talking to her, only to have her beautician gently lower her head back into the sink.

"Marcus, what are you doing here?"

"I came here so we can talk," said Marcus looking around. "I can wait until your finished, then we'll-"

"We're not going anywhere together," Dominique said flatly. "Besides these people are like family, we can talk here."

Marcus glanced at the beautician doing Dominique's hair. She smiled, and as quickly as she smiled the smile disappeared, leaving a complacent expression on her face.

Marcus explained. "I feel awkward doing this, but there is a perfectly good explanation for your confusion. I'm sorry but the earrings you found were Monique's. And you know she is a good friend of mine."

"No need of dragging Monique into this Marcus," said Dominique as she was raised upright by her beautician with a towel wrapped around her head. "Your right you're sorry. Your sorry and trifling!"

"You tell him girlfriend!" shouted a woman sitting under a hair dryer.

"You stay out of this," said Marcus turning to face her.

The woman sitting under a hair dryer continued. "All you sorry ass brothers are the same. Wannabe players, Mack daddies, or whatever ya'll call yourselves. That shit is old. It is old and played out like your sorry ass. Find out what being responsible for your actions and being monogamous is about and maybe she'll stay with your cute ass instead of kicking you to the curb."

Everyone in the salon exploded in a wave of laughter as Marcus turned around and looked at Dominique with pleading eyes.

"Please..."

She put her finger to her lips. "Shhh, begging is so unbecoming of you. I loved you more than you can imagine. I loved you with generous love as a mother, sweet love as a lover, relentless love as a sister, realistic love as a friend, faithful love as a black woman, strong love as a woman, and pure love as Dominique. But there was no love for me in return. Honestly, you lusted for me more than you loved me or I would have been able to move in a long time ago. Face it Marcus, we're better off without each other."

She rose out of her seat as her beautician led her to a dryer and set the controls as Dominique sat down.

"Thanks for coming. I know you're serious because you would have never put yourself in a position like this unless it proved beneficial," said Dominique, looking around at all the attentive eyes on her.

"He thought he could gain our sympathy and convince you to go back with him, girlfriend," said the woman sitting under a hair dryer. "But what he didn't know is how many other sorry ass brothers have came in here and played the same role. Your slippin playa!"

Everyone in the salon exploded in bursts of laughter again as Marcus ignored the women's' comments and looked at Dominique.

"Baby, I still have feeling for you, but you hurt me. I need some space to think okay? Friends?" She held out her hand.

Marcus sighed loudly and reluctantly shook her hand. "Can I call you?"

"I'll call you." She smiled.

Turning away, Marcus slowly walked out of the salon as women stole glances at him and giggled amongst themselves as he walked by.

Stopping at the door, he turned and looked at Dominique for the last time. Then he walked out of the salon as everyone erupted in laughter.

24

PIERRE

Pierre had seen a lot of Michelle that week, enough to know he was feeling the same emotions of when he first met his wife-he was falling in love with her. She didn't seem to mind. It was nice; she said to have a friend to show all sights to, it made a change.

They rented a car and drove all around Miami, visiting places the tourists never seen. She showed him all the places she partied, dined, and the nice, secluded, places where she would go sometimes to watch the sun set over the ocean.

One evening they popped over to her favorite Japanese restaurant "Mori Mori" for dinner.

Tonight they arranged to meet at Casa, a seafood diner off the beach side front.

"I won't be able to do this next week," she said as they prowled between the tanks, sorting out what to eat. "I'm on the schedule for the return flight to Atlanta."

He felt a twinge of pain. Not disappointment, pain. Life with Michelle was...well, just that life. He felt alive again when he was with her.

126

"I'm sorry," he said. "When will we be able to meet again?"

"You'll be back in Atlanta by then," she said. "I'll have three days off then."

"I'm going to miss you," he said, gazing into her eyes.

She smiled sweetly, but he couldn't tell what she really felt.

"You're a busy man," she said. "You'll find a way to kill the time."

Dinner came. For the most part, they ate in silence. Every time Pierre thought of something to say it struck him as otiose; making small talk for the sake of it. Michelle had no need of small talk. She was a self-contained person, he observed. Perhaps she didn't want a man in her life. So it surprised him when, after dinner, she said, "Have you got time to come and visit my place? We could walk, it's not far from here."

"Okay," said Pierre as he thought to himself, *oh, yes my dear; time stands still when I'm with you.*

The apartment was nice, as she put it, but comfortable. Elegant and plush with antique furnishings, matching mirrors, and thick, soft carpet and rugs. A fully stocked bar in the living room next to a patio door that opens to the balcony showing a spectacular view of the city.

While she made drinks, he stepped onto the balcony, curious to see the beach from her view, while lovers walked barefooted, hand in hand, on the beachfront. He stood watching them, as if they might give him a sign. But then she crept up to slip an arm through his; He turned, startled, but already raising his other hand to her face, and so they had their first kiss, on the balcony of her apartment.

She stepped back, looking him over from head to toe.

"Better come in," she whispered. "Drinks are ready."

While he was outside, Michelle had placed soft, scented candles around the small living room and put on some jazz. She went to get the drinks off the bar. He deliberately chose the love seat to sit on, and when she handed him his drink, patted the cushion beside him. For a few minutes they sat there, listening to the music. He wanted so much to kiss her again; He felt different with her, and the notion of simply taking her into his arms excited him.

She put her glass down on the table and sat, half turned to him. She reached out to embrace him, at the same time he slowly leaned toward her. As he moved for the kiss, his hand could scarcely avoid brushing against her leg. She shuddered, a whimper escaped her lips, and he kissed her into silence.

"Why?" He said at last, withdrawing gently.
"Why what?"
"Why this wonderful luck? What have I done that God should make me so happy?"
"You make your own karma," she said quietly. "Perhaps that is why I want you."
"Do you want me?"
She smiled again, and at first he thought that was all the answer he'd get. But then she said, "Your different. I don't know any men like you."
"But surely...."
She shook her head. "Men here have a lot of cavemen in them. Not a brain between them, crazy about sports, and no manners."
"And me?"
"Everything I've ever wanted to find in a man and..."

"Yes?"

She shrugged. "You're you. That's all."

They stayed on the love seat for about thirty minutes. He didn't know what to do, really. He wanted her; she was saying as plain as a body could speak that she was his, she wanted him too. But this was not anything he'd experienced before. This was special.

He was uncertain to ask her to make love to him, so in the end it was she who sat up and said, "Come to bed".

"But what about the candles?"

"Come."

****

She took him by the hand and led him to the bedroom. Returning to the living room to get their drinks, she found him undressed with only his boxers and T-shirt on, sitting on the bed listening to the stereo.

"You really are a romantic, aren't you?"

"You once said I was the deepest person you knew," he said. "My romantic tendencies show this side. Can I play this CD?"

He was holding up the Isley Brothers Greatest Hits. She nodded.

He put the CD on and they listened to it together. When the song, "Spend the Night" started to play, he reached over to turn it down, but she put her hand on his and stopped him.

"Why won't you say what you're feeling?"

WANTING EYES

He shifted nervously and shrugged. It was making him un-
comfortable and embarrassed. It was too close to his feelings,
words that he wanted to say but couldn't. He waited a minute,
then turned the volume down.

"I have a surprise for you," she said, going to the bathroom
and pulling a small bottle of oil off the shelf. "I'm gonna give
you a massage."
"This looks kinky, he said with an expectant grin, as he
quickly undressed.

He had a smooth, well-defined, muscular chest. She liked
that. She had an almost uncontrollable urge to rub his chest with
her hands and wrap herself around him.

Instead she got up and opened the shades to let the moonlight
set the scene. Sitting on the side of the bed, she pulled the covers down to his buttocks, pushing the sheets as far as she could
with decency. She poured a tiny amount of oil on her hands;
rubbed them together and began massaging his back with an almost professional smoothness that came from being massaged
many times over the years.

She did this for about ten minutes until he began to moan and
she realized that she was about to explode from sexual tension
and desire. Finally he turned over and grabbed her wrists.

"I can't stand this anymore, Michelle," he said. His face was
flushed. "Why are you taking care of me?"
She couldn't stand it anymore either.
"Because I love you, Pierre."

It had been that simple to say. He pulled her to him and began to kiss her softly on the mouth, then more passionately,

130

slowly sliding his tongue in her mouth. She thought she would faint. The energy had been drained out of her and she nearly went limp. All the dreams she had had about this moment drifted away as she allowed herself to be touched and held and loved by Pierre.

She realized that she needed desperately to be pleasured by him, to be filled by him and his love, emotionally, intellectually, and especially physically. She needed to let it happen, to let him take charge, to have him make love to her the way he talked to her. She needed to take it all in. Later, then next time, she could participate, but this time she wanted to be taken by him, belong to him completely, and the only way that could happen was to let him do it. Break his shell of uninhibited desire and love her the only way he knew how. Later there would be time for her involvement. Now she wanted only to give herself completely to Pierre.

He didn't disappoint her. How did he know to kiss her and lick her softly on her neck and shoulders until she wanted to scream? Most men weren't that subtle. The pressure of his fingers on the rest of her body was perfect, gentle and eager at the same time. He knew exactly what to do with his tongue and hands, and as he licked her everywhere with his tongue moving slowly down her body until he rested between her legs, she could hear herself as if she were in another room, letting out little moans and gasps of pleasure. He was literally playing her body like a musical instrument. She had never known what that meant. Now, as he tasted her love, she was so excited for him she came in a series of orgasms, likes rushes of heat and electricity passing through her over and over again. She was paralyzed with pleasure. She couldn't make a sound, and only when she stopped shaking did she remember to breathe again.

They lay together quietly enter twined in each other's arms for a long time. She was the one who spoke first.

"Had you only kissed me and not made love to me, Pierre!"
He reached over and brought her to him, enclosing her in his arms.

"Oh, Michelle," he whispered.
"Say you love me," she said.
"I love you."

It was then that she felt the rush of emotion and it surprised her when the tears started in her eyes. She flung herself against his chest and buried her face in it, only realizing after several minutes that the tears were not all hers.

WANTING EYES

They slept for a few hours, woke within of each other, and made love again. It was even better for them this time than it had before; slower and sweeter, with an even graceful and fulfilling rhythm. Michelle was slim, supple, taut, and she took enormous and intense pleasure in her physical condition, drew satisfaction from each flexing and gentle thrusting and soft lazy grinding of their bodies together. It made her feel feminine, healthy, and alive.

With Michelle enjoying the moment, she let hands roam over Pierre's body, marveling over his leanness, testing his rock, hard muscles of his shoulders and arms, kneading the bunched muscles of his back, glorying in the smoothness of his skin, the rocking motion of his hips against hers, pelvis to pelvis, the hot touch of his mouth, her throat, her breasts.

Until this interlude with Pierre, Michelle had not made love in almost fifteen months. And never in her life had she made love like this; never this good, this tender or exciting, never this satisfying.

Finally spent, they lay in each other's arms for a while, basking in the soft afterglow of lovemaking.

"I want to tell you something," Pierre implored, his eyes looking longingly at her.

"Don't," she insisted, putting her hand to his lips to silence him. "Please...I couldn't bear losing you."

"You won't lose me," he said.

"Okay." She hugged and kissed him, then snuggled close to his warm body.

He continued. "There was someone in my life, someone that I tried hard to believe would be the significant other in my life, until I met you. I want you to be a part of my life, because without you there will be no me. My love for you is so pure, so perfect, it reaches out and touches you and brings us together, not only physically, but also with our mind and mostly our souls. Never before has my soul rested from this endless search for love - until now. I want you to live with me, and together lets walk down this path of true love together, hand in hand.

Michelle looked into his eyes and saw sincerity and compassion, a wanting that only one that has found true love can look.

"Well," she said. "We both have had our share of difficulties and struggles. I think we should take each step in our relationship slowly, one day at a time. We'll continue to live separately until we're comfortable enough to start living with each other, okay?"

He nodded.

"We'll just have to decide whose apartment we'll be spending the weekend in."

They both laughed as they tossed the covers over their heads and played mischievously under the sheets.

25

MARCUS

The next four weeks were hectic and busy for Marcus. Not only did his clientele increase, but also one of his many interviews with various companies paid off with Ebony Male, a prominent black magazine, stating that they wanted to see a well-rounded array of photos from him. Ecstatic, he hurriedly jotted down notes from his answering machine and printed out the voice mail sent by the company.

He spent hours going over every photo that he thought would make an impression and added to his portfolio. Everything that he did from a child when his mother purchased his first camera came to this moment that was his dream and he was ambitiously inclined to have come true.

So much in fact that his love life was put on hold. Not that he had an option; he had exhausted all possibilities of even having one. No one of the female persuasion called him, not even Monique. Not that they wanted or had the need to. He had hurt then, not only emotionally but also, mentally. The bridge that he had burnt between them was destroyed, irreversibly unable to be repaired. He knew it deep in his heart so he didn't try to call and left things the way they were.

Except Monique.

He wondered why she hadn't called. Not only were they lovers she was his best friend and that surprised him the most when calls he placed on her answering machine were not returned. She probably found and man and doesn't want to see me in fear of jeopardizing their relationship, he thought as he poured over photos, looking at them with the utmost scrutiny. I probably scared her away with the conversation we had at that cafe.

The annoying buzzing of his office door interrupted his thoughts. He glanced at the clock on the wall. Ten thirty. *Who could be coming over at this time?* He wondered as he rose off his stool and went around a partition.

He stood looking at a silhouette stand at the door. Walking to the door, he slightly parted the blinders to see who was there.

Monique.

"Come on Marcus, open the door, I see you looking," she said with a slight grin.
He opened the door as Monique sauntered in.
"Hey baby, how have you been?" She inquired politely as she kissed him on the cheek.
He shut the door behind her, locked it, and turned facing her.

"How have I been?" He snapped. "How have you been? I've called and left messages, Email you, and even wrote a couple of letters. I was worried about you and you don't even try to ease my fears by answering, but now you feel you can just grace me with you presence like everything is cool and it's not!"

136

"I needed some time to think and mostly you needed time," she countered. "Besides my absence proves opportunity for you."

He shot her a look. She shrugged.

"I'm only repeating the great philosophy of Marcus Jackson," she taunted as she walked over to his table where various photos were scattered about

.

"Busy?"
"Yes, very busy, so if you would mind I would like to continue my work."
"Don't tell me that you're still upset about what we talked about last time?" She observed.
"Not really. It doesn't hurt when you tell someone how you feel and they blow you off," he explained sarcastically as he motioned her upstairs.

As they walked upstairs, Monique explained. "I'm sorry, but I felt I wasn't ready and if my answer didn't suit you, you'd be hurt. So rather than answer, I just placed the question back on you to think about."
She went and sat on the love seat as Marcus went to the kitchen.

"Would you like some wine?" He suggested.
"No, thank you."
"It's your favorite chardonnay."
She shook her head.
"Do you have any juice?"
"Yes."
"That would be nice."

He poured her a glass of apple juice and himself a glass of Chateau St. Jean, then walked over and hand her the drink as he made himself comfortable beside.

"I'm sorry I snapped at you, but I missed you and I was thinking about you and at that moment, you came. I'm sorry."
"It's okay. I apologize too, I should have called."
They tapped their drink and drank.
"Now I have something to tell you that is going to affect both our lives," she said.
"Is it good or bad?"
"Depends on how you take it."

He looked at her and smiled, as if to acknowledge her to continue.

She explained. "The reason I haven't called was I have some major changes going on in my life that needed some soul searching, and in my body that I needed to get adjusted to."

He glanced at her with a confused distraught expression on his face.

She continued. "Marcus, I'm pregnant with your baby. I know it is yours because even though I was dating, you were taking care of my needs so I didn't have to bed every guy I was dating. I didn't want to call cause I was unsure if I want to keep the baby or not, but mostly I was unsure how you would take it. I decided to keep the baby and if you want to be a part of the baby's life it is up to you. So many emotions have flowed through me that I've laughed and cried, but the one thing that made me come here tonight is what you said that day at the cafe. I don't know if you really meant what you said, so that's why I'm here."

She looked at his face, searching for an expression or a sign that could put her at ease, the he understood what she said, but couldn't find anything.

Suddenly his face burst into a glow of happiness and a smile so wide it showed all his teeth. His eyes danced with joy as he reached over ever so slowly and rubbed her stomach and kissed her, passionately with wanton desire.

Then suddenly as he smiled, he rose off the love seat and half stumbled, half ran upstairs to the loft. Monique sat confused and befuddled on the love seat as she watched him run back and forth upstairs.

"Marcus, are you okay?"

Her question was answered with loud noises Marcus made rummaging through his closets. He came stumbling back downstairs and plopped down on the love seat, breathing hard.

"Baby, what's wrong?" She asked.

She started to say something, but he silenced her by putting his fingers over her lips. He took a long sip of wine, caught his breath, and looked into her eyes. She saw a longing, a wanting in his eyes that she had never seen before.

Finally Marcus spoke. "I am the happiest man on earth. I can hardly explain or contain the joy that flows from my heart. Monique, I love you. Never before has those words spoken from my mouth has been said to anyone. I have for the first time in my life found what I can truly love - I have found you. You've always been standing close when I needed you, and feeling me when I needed to be felt. As a friend, you shared the sunshine and the shadows of my day. As a lover, you filled me with love and strength when the world seemed like too much to handle. Because of you, I've learned the true meaning of love, and it wasn't until after we talked at the cafe, I realized it. You're my dreams come true. When I say I love you it's for real and forever and I would love to spend the rest of my life with you and our baby."

He kneeled down on one knee and pulled a small velvet case with gold inscription on it from behind his back. He opened it and the most beautiful two-carat diamond ring sparkled and danced in her teary eyes. As tears flowed down her cheeks he continued. "Monique will you marry me? I want to be with you and you only. Marry me and lets walk down the road of life, hand in hand, in love."

She cried as he gazed at her, waiting for an answer, a gesture, as sign that would put his heart to rest. She finally spoke.

"Baby, I love you so much, but I know how you used to be. If you changed like you said, you'll understand me when I say I'll have to think about it. I'm sorry, but I feel so confused I don't know what I should do."

She rose from the love seat and left him on bended knee, his head in his hand, unknowing that tears fell from his eyes.

PIERRE

The two beautiful weeks Pierre spent with Michelle was the most wonderful time he had in a long time, almost reminiscent of the times spent with his beloved wife. He felt young, vibrant, and most of all there wasn't a guilty bone in his body. Almost as if the love shared by his late wife and him was relived through Michelle. He knew somehow, through destiny's course, love reached out and touched his heart. Michelle had come onto his life, walked into all he had, and showed him simply that also had something beyond this existence, something that he and Kim shared - the sheer happiness of being near each other in a love that was meant to be.

****

At last he returned home, but his happiness was abruptly shortened by the situation Rob as in with his wife. Not only did he occupy his apartment, but also it was transformed from a clean, efficient abode to a letter and dirty clothes strewn, Euro-style bachelor's pat.

Rob sure knows how to make his self at home, Pierre thought as he made his way past the snoring lump on the couch, and stepped carefully past boxes of uneaten pieces of pizza and opened soda cans.

He made his way to the kitchen, turned on the light, and was disgusted at the mess his kitchen was in. Opened cans and microwaveable food wrappers decorated the table and counters. Dirty dishes lay growing in the sink. The trash can swelled over with garbage and poured onto the kitchen floor.

Pierre shook his head as he walked to the refrigerator and opened it. It was empty except for six bottles of Perrier water. After being married as long as he has, he won't survive as a bachelor, Pierre thought as he took a bottle of water and walked into his study to check his Email messages.

His routing mail was in and waiting for responses or replies, but he was looking for a message or something from Michelle letting him know her whereabouts. Nothing. He logged off and sighed, turned, and went to his room to get some sleep. Looking at Rob dozing on the couch, he made up his mind to help Rob make up with Marie before his apartment gets totaled.

****

The next morning Pierre awoke abruptly to the high pitch wail of the vacuum cleaner. Rob was cleaning. He glanced sleepily at the clock. Eleven- thirty. He was still tired, but quite rested for the moment. He just wants to lie in and reminisce over the time he spent with Michelle, but he knew the noise would overwhelm him to the point he had to get up.

He rose from bed and went to the bathroom to wash up. *The first thing I have to do today is help Rob make up with Marie,* he thought as he washed his face. *I have to get my place back.*

He quickly brushed his teeth and changed into something casual, then went into the living room. It was spotless except for an unmade makeshift bed on the couch.

The shattering of dishes hitting the floor startled him. As he walked into the kitchen Rob was kneeling, picking up pieces of scattered glass.

"I think you better put on your slippers till I sweep this up," Rob said, glancing up at Pierre with an embarrassed look on his face. "I'm sorry."

"It's okay," Pierre said as he turned and went back into his room, put on his slippers and returned. "I'll just put it on your hotel bill."

Rob smiled. He continued. "How long have you bee staying here?"

"About three weeks," Rob mumbled as he continued picking up glass.

Pierre retrieved a broom and dustpan from a small closet and started sweeping. "Is it that bad?"

143

"I don't think so, we've been working it out slowly."
"And...."
"We're making progress, but it's a touchy situation."

Pierre returned the broom to the closet as Rob threw away the glass. Placing the dustpan in the closet, Rob sat down at the table as Pierre poured a cup of coffee for him, then himself as he sat down. Rob sighed and rubbed his forehead as Pierre sipped his coffee and looked at him.

"Thanks man, for letting me stay. You don't know how much I appreciate it."
    Pierre shook his head and raised his hand. "You're my best friend, it's the least I could do"
"So how was your trip?" Rob asked.
"Beautiful. I met the most wonderful woman."
"Really? Do tell and don't leave anything out."

So Pierre started to tell Rob from when he met Michelle and didn't leave anything out till they parted. When he finished, Rob was smiling broadly. "I'm so happy for you. Now if I can find a way to ignite the flame of love in me and Marie's relationship, I'll be as happy as you. Any suggestions?"

"Rob, you know the love is not lost in your relationship, the flame is just burning low," Pierre reassured him. "What you have to do is stoke the flame, and to stoke it you have to go back to the basics. You have to court your wife, woo her, and show her the good time you and her had, before the marriage, kid, and career when you were lovers. And it just doesn't stop when you win her back. You have to continue to keep the romance in your marriage. That's it. Words don't mean a thing if actions don't take precedence in the matter. They will be just that - words."

Rob nodded as he continued. "Romance never dies in a relationship, you just exhaust the possibilities."

Rob smiled and held out his fist as Pierre gave him a pound.

"You know what? Everything my wife did I took for granted, and I didn't realize it till I'm away from her. Thanks for the advice man. I'm just glad you're happy."

"What are friends for? I'm only helping a man that helped me help myself. Now handle your business so I can get my place back." Together they laughed as Pierre poured some more coffee for him.

****

Some time later that evening, Pierre was relaxing comfortably in his love seat, soaking up some smooth sounds of Maze as the phone rang. He picked it up after three rings.

"Hello?"
"Hey baby, you miss me?"

Michelle.

"Like crazy. I've been doing stupid things like writing your name with my last name on paper over and over again. I'm constantly thinking about you. I miss you, baby. I miss your kiss, your touch, your smell, and your sheer essence. Other than that, I've had a pretty laid back day."

"Thinking of marriage already, huh? I put it on you that bad?"
"Not bad enough, I think I need another fix."
She laughed. "What if I told you that I'd be off for the next three days?"
"I'd have to say I would love to spend it with you."
"Wouldn't have it any other way."
"See you then tomorrow?"
"I'll call before coming, bye."

"Bye." Pierre hung up with a sheer sense of overwhelming happiness that he had to contain himself from shouting. He was so happy and preoccupied with his thoughts that it startled him when the doorbell rang. Thinking Rob forgot his keys, he shouted, "I should let you go home and face Marie for this!"

He walked to the door and opened it. To his surprise Sandra stood there quietly and looking as beautiful as ever. She was dressed in a jet-beaded plunge V-neck top and wool crepe wide leg pants that hugged her body and showed her curvaceous body. Her natural sandy red hair was tousled, making her look incredibly sexy. She stood paused, as if waiting for a sign, but when Pierre walked towards her, she hugged him tentatively, as if not wanting to let him go.

Sandra spoke first. "I missed you."
"I missed you too, you look good."
"Thank you."

He motioned her in and shut the door behind her as she sauntered over and sat in the love seat. Pierre took a place nearest her on the couch. Sandra looked at him and patted on the love seat beside her. When he shook his head, she knew something was up.

"What's wrong?"
"We have to talk."
"I know," she added. "But let me get something off my chest first, it's been a long time coming."
"Okay."
She continued. "Pierre, I know my behavior probably has pushed you away from me, and if you don't wish to be with me I understand."
"Nothing you can say will change how I feel about you at this moment," Pierre reassured her.

Sandra explained. "For four years I was in an abusive relationship, both mentally and physically. My husband, Terry, at first was a wonderful lover, but as soon as we were married, he became very possessive and jealous. If I were late from work we'd argue and fight. Later he would apologize and I thought he'd stop, but it continued.

Tears swelled in Sandra's eyes and spilled down her cheeks as she pushed herself on. "Then the cheating started. At first I didn't want to believe it, till one night when he was suppose to be on a business trip, I caught him with another woman. When we divorced, he left me penniless and without a home, but it was fine, I just wanted my freedom. But that sick relationship had me believing that was love until I lost friends from mistrust and being demanding of time and money. Until I met you..." She smiled at him, as he looked her with genuine concern and sympathy in his eyes. "You made me realize that there are caring sensitive, tender, loving men that want true love in their lives. From that realization, I tried to win you over the best way I knew how. When all the while I was pushing you away, for that I apologize."

Pierre rose from the sofa and sat down beside her and took her hand. "Sandra you are a very beautiful woman, and if it wasn't for your love at that point and time in my life, I don't know where I would have been. We needed each other physically and mentally, and for that you will always be a friend I can confide in." Pierre leaned towards Sandra and kissed her on the cheek, and then they hugged.

"I've never felt so completely in love with this woman I met, and I owe it all to you, thank you," he whispered in her ear.
Tears streamed down Sandra's cheek as she closed her eyes. More importantly she realized that Pierre would never look at her the way he did after that night they made love.

"I'm happy for you, Pierre," Sandra sighed, running her fingers thru his hair. "Tell your lady friend she snagged a definite keeper."

She squeezed him tight one last time, then forced herself to let him go. Rising from the love seat, she took him by the hand and together they walked to the door.

"I guess this is it, huh?" She held out her hand. "Best friends?"
He shook her hand then, raising it palm down, kissed her on the back of her hand.

"Forever."

"I see you haven't lost your touch," Sandra purred, blushing as she walked away.
Pierre watched her walk away as a lone tear streamed silently down his cheek. He wiped his face, sighed, and closed the door.

27

ROB

It had been two weeks since Rob had seen Marie, not because he was avoiding her, but because she chose not to see him. She left Christian over her parent's house so he could see his son and curt notes telling him she was either busy or working. But tonight whether she chose to or not she was going to see him. He thought long and hard on what it would take for his wife to love him the way they used to love each other, the way she used to look at him with the longing and love in her eyes that as only for him to see. And with Pierre's advice, he had found a way. Prepared to do whatever it took, he drove to his house.

It had been a mistake from the start, compromising the love he and his wife shared for an affair that led to nothing but misery and disappointment. He realized, now more than ever, that the love his wife has was strong, fulfilling love, and he took it for granted. And with him, taking her love for granted, he lost the one thing that his marriage was nourished on - romance. It was gone, and without it, the once burning flame of love was reduced to a small glowing ember. But now he was willing to chance everything to gain that love back in his wife's eyes and in their relationship. You never realize how good a love was until it's missing from your life; he thought was he turned up in his driveway behind his wife's Honda Civic.

He walked up to the door and rang the doorbell. He didn't want to use his keys because he wanted his surprise to be formal as possible. The porch light came on, and then the door opened. His wife stood, looking at him in surprise, her hands on her hips.

He had dressed exquisitely for the occasion, with a blue Versace pinstriped, two button double breasted side vent suit jacket with matching pants, a cotton honeycomb button down placket front dress shirt, and some black Giorgio Britain shoes. Behind his back, he held a bouquet of yellow carnations, her favorite.

"What brings you here looking all handsome stranger?" Marie inquired politely.

Rob explained. "I come to you, my love, as a bee thirsts for honey, for you to accompany me to dinner, and whatever the night has to offer, the night is young."
"But I'm not even dressed," Marie replied. "Maybe another time, Rob."
"I cannot waste another minute being without you, Marie," he pleaded. "Please play along and get dressed."
"Ooh, I love it when a handsome man begs," purred Marie. "I'll get dressed."
"Before you get dressed," Rob added, "I brought you these." He brought his arm from behind his back and produced a beautiful bouquet of yellow carnations.

Marie gasped and covered her mouth with her hands. It had been a while since Rob had brought her flowers, more little anything for that matter. She took the carnations and smelled them as Rob kissed her on the cheek.

"Rob, they're beautiful!" She exclaimed.

"Oh? I haven't noticed," he stated. "Beside you they have lost their beauty."

She looked up at him and saw the sincerity and love in his eyes, then quickly turned away. She didn't want to give in that easy, at least not yet.

"I better get dressed," she suggested.

She went to the kitchen and put the flowers in the water, then retired to the bathroom to shower and change.

Within an hour or so, she was dressed and ready. She went to the living room and paused in the doorway for Rob to see her. She looked absolutely stunning.

She wore a black bias top with net sleeves that showed her slender shoulders, and a charcoal skirt with side slits and sequin detailing that showed her sexy thighs. High stiletto pumps accented her outfit and made her calves look full. Her hair cascaded from her head to her shoulders in waves and curls.

A whimper escaped Rob's lips as he gazed upon his wife as she walked before him and posed. He hurriedly rose to his feet as she walked by.

"How do I look?" She asked, spinning around.

"Absolutely beautiful," he observed, unable to take his eyes off her. "I hope the gods don't mind a mere mortal taking out one of their goddesses."

Marie giggled. She hadn't dressed up or felt this giddy since the first time they met.

152

"Are you ready?" He asked.   He held out his hand.

She nodded as she put her hand in his. Together they walked to the door as he opened it and allowed her to pass through. Hurrying to the passenger side of the car he opened the door for her, waited till she was comfortable, then closed it and hurriedly walked to the driver side and got in.

He turned and looked at Marie, then took her hand. "I hope this is the beginning of a new chapter in the love of our life."

"So far so good," Marie reassured him.

He pulled out of the driveway and drove into the night. The night was clear and dark, like a dark velvet shroud, except for a few stars sparkling and winking, like photographers were taking their pictures for the world to see.

They finally pulled up to the Déjà' Vu, an exquisite African restaurant known for it's down home soul food and live jazz. As the maitre de showed them to their table and gave menus, Marie took Rob's hand into hers.

"If you're just doing this to make up, I don't want to go through with this," she whispered.
Rob looked into her eyes for a moment, and then lowered his head.
"Baby, I'm doing this for selfish reasons, and if you don't want to stay I'll take you home, but first let me explain."
Marie looked at Rob as he raised his head, and then nodded for him to continue.

Rob explained. "We've been together for a long time and it's always been about me. I've been so selfish and I'm sorry.

153

But if you would accept me back into your life, I promise you that I will be selfish for you and only for you. I want the love we had before our marriage, our son, and my job. I want the love that we had when we were careless and free. And for that I'm willing to do anything - for you." He started to continue, but was stopped by Marie putting two fingers to his lips.

"Shhh, I understand," She reassured him. "Let's enjoy this moment."

The waiter brought them some wine and the maitre de uncorked it and poured it into their glasses. After informing them that their entrees will be ready soon and if they needed anything don't hesitate to raise a hand, the maitre de left their table. Rob raised his glass and took Marie's hand in his other hand.

"I would like to toast this night to romance," he said. "May the spirits of romance tonight enchant my beautiful wife into my arms, and may I never lose sight on the love I have for you."

Marie raised her glass and Rob started to tap it with his glass to seal the toast but she stopped him.

"What's wrong?" Rob asked.

"I'd like to make a toast too."

"Okay."

She cleared her throat. "I would like to toast you, Rob, for being a man first, realizing your mistakes, and lastly for making a sound decision. I was hurt deeply from what transpired over past weeks, and I thought over and over what I done to drive you away into the arms of another. I realize now it takes two to keep a relationship alive, and we both were guilty of falling into a mundane relationship. That is why I decided to work it out instead of throwing away everything we had accomplished together. But never do this to me again or we'll part under different circumstances."

What she said at that moment was so touching that it left a lump in Rob's throat and tears in his eyes. He wiped his eyes and cleared his throat. "Then this toast is for you baby, for accepting me for my mistakes and being a strong black woman.

She nodded as they tapped glasses and drank.

Dinner came. For the most part they ate in silence, only looking occasionally into each other's eyes and shyly smiling at each other. So it surprised her when Rob rose up and went around to her side of the table and kneeled to one knee. He took her hand into his and kissed it. Then he reached into his suit pocket and produced a small velvet case.

She gasped as Rob spoke. "Marie, you don't know how much I longed for your touch, and your careless whisper that means so much. Your kiss, I long to embrace them heavenly lips, sweet as honey, I long to taste. The sheer smell of you, reminds me of a garden of roses, laden with dew. When I was away from you, these thoughts I reminisced, these precious senses, I truly missed. This longing I wanted, that was so faintly seen, is alive now, recaptured from my dreams. As quiet as kept, deep in our souls, burns a love so strong, a faith so bold, that when the sands of strife, tried to blow us apart, our love burnt stronger, within our hearts. Now our paths have crossed, our destinations complete, for it is my soul mate, my lover, my solace of peace, it is you Marie, that I long to be with."

He opened the velvet case and a sparkling two-carat diamond ring twinkled in her teary eyes. "Baby, would you remarry me? Take this ring as a token of my love and together we'll journey down this road of life, hand in hand, in a renewed love."

Tears poured down her cheeks as she gazed into his eyes. She saw a longing, a wanting of love in his eyes that was only for her to see.

"Yes, baby I do."

The restaurant burst into applause and cheers as Rob gently put the ring on Marie's finger and hugged her. "I love you so much Rob," she whispered in his ear as she hugged him.

"I love you too, baby."

****

Despite the hour, they left the restaurant. As Rob opened the door for Marie and she sat in the car, he looked at her.

"Baby, do you trust me?" He said.
"Do you want me to be honest or lie?"

He shot her a serious look.

"I'm not talking about that, I want you to wear this." He produced a silk scarf from the inside pocket of his suit. "I want you to wear this, I have a surprise for you."
"After what you just did I don't think you can top that."
"Give me a chance." He glanced at her unexpectantly, and then when she nodded, he covered her eyes with the scarf. "Is this too tight?" He asked as he gently tied a knot behind her head and tighten it.
"It's okay."

He shut the car door then hurriedly got in the car. For the most part he drove in silence, reassuring her as she asked end-lessly question after question.

They arrived at the luxurious Four Oaks in downtown At-lanta. A doorman opened Marie's door as Rob and the porter exchanged places.

"I got you baby, you have to trust me," he said, as he helped her out of the car and gently led her into the hotel. He made her sit in one of their plush sofas in the lobby as he went to the re-ceptionist desk.

157

"Is everything ready?" Rob inquired politely as the receptionist gave him the key to his suite.

"Yes sir, everything has been set up as you requested," he said. "If you need anything else, just call the desk. Thank you for staying with us and I hope our accommodations suit you."

"Thank you."

Rob went back to where his wife was sitting impatiently, and helped her to her feet. He led her, through the lobby, to the elevator, and pushed a button. The elevator groaned slightly as it made its way upward.

"Are we there yet?" Marie said flatly. "I want to take this scarf off."

"We're almost there," Rob reassured her. "Be patient baby."

The elevator made a gentle stop and with a ring opened its doors. Leading her to the suite, Rob opened the door and escorted her in.

"Please," Marie replied. "I'm anxious I don't think I can take this much longer.

Rob stood behind her and gently untied the scarf. He pulled it off as Marie opened her eyes.

To her surprise she stood in a lush presidential suite. The long flowing curtains were pulled back, showing Atlanta's skyline besetted by a starry sky. Small scented candles lighted her path and around her feet, yellow carnations petals were strewn about, making a path to the bedroom.

Marie gasped as Rob led her to the bedroom where lighted scented candles were everywhere. Near the bed was a tray where a bottle of champagne lay chilled next to two crystal

158

glasses. A small shrine of candles were on the beautifully carved inlaid oak dresser, and in the midst of the candles was a wedding picture they had taken a long time ago.

"Rob, this is too much!" She exclaimed. "How much did you spend to arrange this?"

She walked around the room, then turned facing him.

"This is nothing compared to the love I have for you," he replied. "I just want to romance you the way you deserved to be romanced. From this day forward, your man will be different from anything you have experienced from me in the past." He walked towards her, hugged her tentatively, and started kissing her on the neck. "I want to be your friend, brother, father, and most of all, your lover, that will tend to your needs and desires as only I know how."

He turned her around and kissed her lightly on her neck as he slowly unzipped her blouse.
"But...."
He swung her around by the shoulders and slowly pulled the straps off her shoulders. Her top fell to the ground, exposing her breasts.
"No buts. When I walked through that door it was the last time you'll ever see the old Rob."

He kissed her into silence as he slowly undressed her. She lay back on the yellow carnation bed petal covered bed, naked except of her earrings and her gold clasped waist let around her. He walked over to the bedside where a small aphrodisiac kit in a small wicker basket lay. He picked up a small bottle of honey-scented oil and poured copious amounts in his hand. With his other hand, he lifted her left foot, holding the heel in the palm of his hand. He rubbed the oil into the instep, sole and ankle, and in between each toe. Then the other foot. Then both legs until they were oily and smooth, sliding backward and forwards with his hands as they moved up her body.

"Is this nice?" He asked.

"Mmm." Her eyes closed and she smiled as he massaged her slowly, working his way up her body. His right hand found her love as his left hand massaged her breasts and her waist. She reached out with her right hand towards his mouth. He licked her fingertips as he teased her love. She gasped as his tongue flicked between her circling fingers. His hands stretched up to her breasts, pinching her erect nipples as she led him down to her love with her hand and gripped his head with her thighs. She held him down by the hair as she shuddered, succumbing to wave after wave of orgasms, coursing through her body like electricity. He slowly rose, kissing his way upward as he went, on her thighs, her navel, her breasts, her neck.

He groaned slightly as he entered her. All the passion that was built up for this moment spread like a blanket of electricity, joining them on a plane of ecstasy never felt.

They made love well into the wee hours of the morning. For them it was a confirmation of their love anew from the episode that caused them much discontent and confusion within the sanctity of their marriage. Time was forgotten as their bodies lay enter twined, pressed together in the age old rhythm of love, as passion met love and desire, encircling them in a haze of heat. That night, it seemed they could make love forever.

SEVEN YEARS LATER......

28

A fine breeze floated like pale water over the grass, drifting, eddying, swaying the trees silently, turning them into animated characters, waving as they embraced the sunny sky.

Beyond the grassy field, the Mount Zion Baptist church was visible in the distant, its bell tower obscured by the shimmering light so that only the church and part of the steeple were visible now.

And all about this summer landscape lay an unremitting silence, as if the world had stopped; everything was bathed in a vast unconsciousness. The stillness was all solitude; nothing moved or stirred.

The low meadow beyond the church was verdant and lush with billowing grass, every kind of wildflower grew among the grasses. But on this warm Saturday afternoon in May, they appeared cool and inviting.

Pierre loved this kind of weather, for inevitably it was day-dreaming weather, it brought the past back to him, and happily so, reminded him of years that past. Michelle and Pierre was married in the following year and blessed with a baby boy that they named Jamil.

As he parked his car, then got out and went to the passenger side to escort Michelle and Jamil into the church, the air was warm, the sunshine felt good to his face. Unexpectantly, Michelle got out and hugged him, and kissed him on the cheek. He looked into her eyes and smiled as he closed the door, then opened the rear door and helped Jamil out of his car seat.

As he told her many times, her eyes looked so warm and radiantly filled with love that sometimes it prevented him from speaking. He swallowed the lump that rose in his throat, took her and Jamil by the hand and together, arm in arm, they went into the church.

Today was a very special day, not for Pierre, but for his godson. Christian was eleven and now it was his time, to take up his responsibilities as a young black man. This was the year of his passage from a boy to a man. Mount Zion Baptist church minister was esurient to instill in the young black men of the church the appreciation and understanding with pride of the beauty of the African race, so he instituted the passage as a initiation rite so black males would make that transition to manhood with a sense of discipline and respect.

On his eleventh birthday, Christian called for his passage. This initiative made him take his first step towards responsibility. After his passage date was set, a certain criteria had to be met before his twelfth birthday. He had to keep a log, a record of his transition beginning from the passage year. He had to read at least fifty books and write review of them, to include black periodicals, so he could endeavor to gain understanding and appreciation with pride of beauty of the black race.

He had to gain the understanding of his immediate and extended family by making a full list of relationships and whereabouts of each relative, beginning with his immediate family. He had to service his neighborhood and community in self help services and drives, and adopt a senior citizen to help out occasionally on a weekly basis. This in turn will help him gain an understanding of his responsibilities as a black man, and the discipline to do the right thing.

As Pierre, Michelle, and Jamil, entered the church, they were greeted by Rob and his wife with Christian, and Marcus and Monique with five year old Malikah. They whispered, hugged, and shook hands with one another, as if the church dictated their actions.

The church was silent, except for an occasional murmur from the audience, until the organist took her seat at the organ and played some music to set the mood.

Looking around, Pierre noticed the beauty of the church on this special day. The stained glass that surrounded the walls told the story of the bible through its windows. It was elegant, but somewhat austere, relying on its proportions and simplicity for is intrinsic beauty.

Scanning it quickly, his eyes caught sight of a beautifully African woven tapestry on one wall, and a large framed carved mask on another. Candles like small lamps flicker and paved the way to the altar that was ceremoniously decorated for the occasion. Everyone was exquisitely dressed in traditional African garb.

When the usher greeted them in the lobby and told them that the passage was about to begin, Rob turned and faced Pierre.

"Thanks for doing this for Christian," he stated. "You know he looks up to you the most."

"I know. Just don't make this a habit with the next one," Pierre added, rubbing his wife's belly. "This one will be Marcus' prodigy."

"No, no, no," Monique countered. "Marcus has his hand full already."

Everyone looked at Marcus standing in the nearby corner of the lobby, quietly rocking his daughter to sleep, and smiled.

"That's cute," whispered Michelle, as she nudged Pierre in his side. "When are we going to have another child?"

Pierre shot her a surprised look as Monique nodded in agreement. "Yeah, Pierre. When are you and Michelle planning to have a baby?"

"We're planning," Pierre replied. "And as long as we're planning, its all good."

"How long have you guys been married now?" Monique inquired politely.

"Shhh, it's about to begin," Pierre countered, ignoring Monique's question.

The organist sounded the processional and Christian entered, walked down the isle, and stood beside the minister. His parents followed with Pierre, Michelle, and Jamil. When his parents were halfway down the aisle, Christian walked back and joined his parents up the aisle as Pierre, Michelle, and Jamil, took a seat in the second pew with Monique and Marcus.

The minister, presiding over the ceremony, gave a small talk explaining the meaning of manhood, its obligations, and its responsibility to elders, men, women, children, race, community, and nation. Afterwards he turned and faced Christian.

"Whose manhood do we honor this day," he said.
"Christian Curie."
"Why do you wish to accept the passage to Manhood?"

165

"The time has come and I am ready to accept my responsibilities," replied Christian.

The minister turned and faced the audience. "Do you approve of Christian Curie seeking responsibilities for manhood?"

The audience erupted in a resounding amen.

His parents took seats in the front pew as Christian sat in a
chair facing the minister. Silence fell over the audience like a
blanket as the ceremony began. Marcus kissed Monique on the
cheek, then Malikah, then quietly rose to take pictures.

Daydreaming, Pierre is brought back to reality by his wife
Michelle squeezing his hand. He had always thought that he
could never be happy, since that dreadful day that his late wife
and son were tragically torn from him. Now happiness and love
returned to him, like the sun after a storm brings a rainbow
through the storm clouds. Like a river finds the ocean, he knew
on an instinctual level, that his wife wanted him to love, and to
receive love.

As he turned and kissed Michelle on the cheek, and hugged
Jamil, he noticed Rob looking back at him. He nodded and
smiled.

Rob's marriage sailed through troubled waters with his infi-
delity, but it was through the strong determination of Marie that
his marriage lasted. A black woman's love is magical and special, and he knows now that it shouldn't be taken for granted.

The flash of a camera caught the corner of his eye. There in
a corner with all the lights set up was Marcus, taking pictures of
the ceremony. He shook his head, wondering what made Marcus settle down. But now that he has, he is definitely a family
man. Won't go anywhere without his wife and kid, and spends
endless hours with Malikah. He finally landed a steady gig with

Ebony Male, a prominent black magazine, as a still photographer, photographing well-known models all over the world. Though stints on the job kept them somewhat apart, the quality time is made up for when he returned home. He doesn't even run the streets anymore.

His thoughts were broken as all the men in the audience recited a poem as he joined in. When they finished the women responded by saying amen.

"Baby, you have to speak," said Michelle, nudging him out of his seat.

Pierre rose and went to the podium. The audience fell silent as he cleared his throat.

"Christian, I watched you grow from a beautiful baby that wetted his pants, to the bright, intelligent, young black man that I see before me today. We've grown together, Christian, for I grew with you. Suffering from a great loss you became my solace, and with that I also cared for you like you were my own. Now I charge you, Christian, to be the same inspiration and example not only to others younger than you, but to my son Jamil. So we all may grow together in the understanding of self and others."

Pierre went to his seat as Christian's parents came up and gave words of advice and inspiration to their son. Then Christian rose, acknowledged the minister, his parents and relatives, then recited his speech. When he finished, the minister joined him at the podium.

"Christian Curie, we welcome you the honored realm, challenges, and responsibilities of black manhood."

The audience immediately erupted in cheers and approval. An atmosphere of joy and celebration settled over the crowd as

167

the organist played Lift Every Voice and Sing, as the minister, Christian, and his parents proceeded to the rear of he church.

The ushers excused the congregation pew by pew as they gathered at the rear of the church to shake hands and welcome Christian to manhood.

WANTING EYES

****

Some time later that afternoon, they all gathered at Rob's house for the barbecue. All the ladies gathered around the picnic table and gossiped and laughed as they watched their kids play. Pierre, Marcus, and Rob sat around the grill, instructing Christian how to barbecue.

"The first thing you need to learn is that we like our meat done," teased Marcus, sipping on a beer.

"You're doing fine, Shorty Mack," reassured Pierre, as he helped him turn over the meat.
Michelle and her friends had prepared a truly delicious lunch. There were all manner of delicious and succulent things to eat with the barbecue - potato salad, collard greens, cabbage, red beans and rice, and of course, Pierre's self proclaimed famous mouthwatering jambalaya.

"What do you want on your plate, baby," said Michelle, as she walked around the table, deciding where to start.
"A little bit of everything, baby thanks," replied Pierre.

Rob came out of the house and moved slowly around the table, pouring red champagne. It was bottled in 1989, a good year, and he commented it to Marie, who nodded and smiled.

"Chosen especially for you," Marie told him with a conspiratorial wink.
Marcus followed him, filling the kids glasses with juice; Pierre passed around the basket of homemade cornbread and Christian offered potato chips.

169

At last they were all served, and they settled down to eat. Pierre ate slowly, savoring his food, saying a word or two occasionally. Mostly he listened, and observed everyone. He was very content today, enjoying this respite from his work, being with his family and friends. Part of his family at any rate. He could not help wishing Kim were here, and Jeremy. But he knew they were there with him, in spirit, complete, a true family under one roof. At that moment, the wanting that bore into his heart like a worm burrows into an apple was sated, and he was filled. He rose to his feet, glass in hand.

"I'd like to say something," he declared.

Everyone took their glasses and held them up and gave him their full attention.

"When my wife and son were killed, I thought my life was over. Until two friends of mine stopped me from blaming myself." He glanced at Marcus and Rob as they smiled and nodded.

He continued. "With their help I started trying to live, but it wasn't the same, until I met Michelle. She gave me life in a way that was blessed and I know that Kim, if she's looking down on us right now with Jeremy, will approve. Thanks baby, Rob and Marcus, for being there when I needed you."

Rob slowly rose to his feet and hugged Pierre, then Marcus joined in.

"Thank you for always being there for me," Rob said.
"We've always been down, ain't nothing changed," Marcus said

"Except you," Pierre and Rob said in unison, as they laughed and toasted.

170

Marcus rolled his eyes then laughed. "Oh yeah, the very best of friends, my boys."

They all hugged and laughed, then sat down to eat.

www.ingramcontent.com/pod-product-compliance
Lightning Source LLC
Chambersburg PA
CBHW020615250626
47154CB00004B/1525